FALLING
OUT
of
FOCUS

by

Brynn Myers

Second Edition, 2021
First Printing, 2017
ISBN: 9798598933497

Cover design by Inkstain Designs
Edited by Laura Bruzan

Indigo Ink Publications, Florida

www.brynnmyers.com

Praise for Entasy

"WOW, this prequel/novella has everything that I craved for: action, suspense, mysterious creatures, Celtic legends and myths, sadist bad guy, wonderful and kick-ass female character and of course a bunch of super sexy, yummy, handsome, supernatural hotness! This story was overwhelming and I loved it!" ~ *Proserpine Craving Books*

"This is a series to truly enjoy, you know those books you just can't put down but you don't want it to finish so soon, yes, this is one of them. I would recommend this to those who find themselves interested in books about magic, Celtic mythology, action, suspense and of course, love. Be ready to dive into the world of The Nine and their stories." ~ *Lunar Haven Reviews*

"This is the first book of Brynn Myers I have read and I have to say, I was enchanted from the beginning... This really was an addicting book that I read in less than a day..." ~ *Redheads Review it Better*

Praise for Redemption

"So many elements that kept me glued to every page. Mystery, fantasy, romance, conflict and drama. The main character grown tremendously in the book - LOVE. What sent me over the top in love with Brynn's world was the significance in every detail. I am also a sucker for villains and cliff hanger endings! Well done, Brynn, it's not often a second book in the series can outdo its debut, but this book did, and I was totally satisfied as to how it started and the magnificent ending!" ~ *World Away Book Blog*

"Heartwarming, tear jerking, wonderfully written story. You feel every emotion, while sitting on the edge of your seat as the scene unfolds not only in the book but in your mind as well. I highly recommended the book, it is a great read!!!" ~ *Goodreads Reviewer*

"I was so looking forward to reading this book and I was not disappointed...I could not put this book down as so much was happening that I just kept turning the pages. Plenty of action and the romance was steamy yet sweet at times. Liam was the ultimate baddie, obsessive and cruel yet determined to possess Kylah at whatever the cost. So many twists and turns and I enjoyed reading about Kylah's journey." ~ *Goodreads Reviewer*

Praise for The Life & Death of Jorja Graham

"If you have a penchant for the mystical, for some frightening bits thrown in and for a well plotted, well written book to spend a few hours with... CHOOSE THIS. You won't be disappointed." ~ *Camaro (Goodreads Top Reviewer)*

"This story had everything from romance to things that go bump in the night. The dialogue was eloquently written and flowed effortlessly. The imagery was perfectly detailed. The Life & Death of Jorja Graham is unique, enchanting, and will keep you guessing until the very end. Five Unexpected Stars!" ~ *Brandi (Brandi's Bookshelves)*

"The Life & Death of Jorja Graham has a contemporary romance feel to it in the beginning but has a massive paranormal twist. I give this book 5 stars and I would recommend it to fans of romance, suspense, and paranormal genre fans." ~ *Charity (Literal Addiction)*

"If you enjoy a suspenseful, mysterious, mystical, eerie, and paranormal that comes out of nowhere and surprises you, then this book is for you. I give it 4 stars and cannot wait to read the next book in this series." ~ *Tiffany (NerdGirl Reviews)*

Praise for The Echoed Life of Jorja Graham

"Perfect!! I loved this series so hard! This was the perfect conclusion to one of my favorite paranormals. If you loved book one, The Life and Death of Jorja Graham (which you'll need to read first), you'll love this one even more! The author not only surpassed my expectations, she broadened the playing field and deepened my love for these unforgettable characters. Just when you think it can't get any better, it does! ." ~ *Brandi (Brandi's Bookshelves)*

"Such a detailed, in-depth world. I loved the journey and final conclusion to Jorja's story. The mythology and magic weaved throughout this book is intoxicating! Brynn's writing in flawless! 5 well-deserved stars!!" ~ *Goodreads Reviewer*

"Wow. This book was wonderful! It held my attention just as much as the first book did. I absolutely enjoyed this book. I was unable to put it down. I love books that capture you from the first page to the last, and this book did exactly that." ~ *Goodreads Reviewer*

Acknowledgements

I dedicate this book to anyone who's ever felt, at some point or another in their life, as though they were drowning in a dark abyss. There is a light in there somewhere. Find it and follow it.

I'd also like to thank L.T., this book would never have come to fruition without your support and guidance. Thank you for reminding me it was and is possible!

querencia: (n.) a place from which one's strength is drawn, where one feels at home; the place you are your most authentic self.

Have you ever dreamt about letting go? You know, not caring about the consequences of your choices…just standing on the edge of a proverbial cliff and simply falling? I have. More times than I can count, I'm afraid. Now, before you go thinking I'm talking about suicide, let me clarify, I'm not. This isn't like the scene from *Thelma & Louise*, not even close. I'm talking about looking out into an abyss and mentally free-falling so you no longer have to exist within the normal parameters of the world. Simply becoming one with the universe. Mental freedom in its purest form.

I have had many variations of this dream, but one remains consistent. I'm standing on the edge of that cliff with my arms spread wide as the sun beats down, and a cool breeze blows across my skin. It's then that I let myself fall—flying free into the unknown of my choosing. Today the sky is a rose gold with flecks of silver glinting from the rays of the sun. The grass beneath my feet is a vibrant green and the sea a stunning mixture of cobalt and teal. I stare out at the vastness of the water and guess the point where the ocean and the sky became one. It's peaceful in this dream. I guess that's why I always come back, hoping like Dorothy or Alice that I'll find my own version of Oz or Wonderland...and luckily, today is that day.

It was 5:45pm when I decided my future.

By 9:43 I was well on my way to making it all come true.

At 11:16 I took the first step to make it a reality.

At 11:17 I fell and found peace.

Chapter One

The air went from warm to cool as I fell from the sunlight into the darkness. I was sliding down a black hole that felt smooth and slick, as if I was slipping on marble. The vortex was swirling downwards towards the earth and there were no sounds to distinguish where I was or where I was heading— only silence.

Down.

Down.

Down.

The sensation that followed left me gasping for air. I couldn't breathe. The water around me was freezing and it felt as if my bones were going to snap from the pressure.

"Breathe," a voice inside my head screamed.

"How? I'm underwater."

"You can."

A moment later, I'd managed to kick myself to the surface. A rush of air hit my face, and I coughed and sputtered as I tried to catch my breath.

"Excuse me!" a voice exclaimed. "Do you normally just intrude upon people in such an intrusive way? Where are your manners?"

I went to speak but was lacking clear thought. There before me stood an otter dressed in a three-piece suit and a bowler hat which was now spotted with water. He looked like he'd just stepped out of an episode of Downton Abbey.

"I'm…I'm sorry?" I choked.

"Oh yes, indeed. I can tell by the sincerity in your voice just how sorry you are," the otter snapped as he took off his hat and used a handkerchief to wipe it.

"I think I bumped my head."

"That's the excuse for your rudeness?" He huffed and put his hat back on then turned his attention to the mud that had tipped his shoes.

I closed my eyes and shook my head in hopes of clearing my thoughts. This dream had gone awry for sure.

"Are you ill or something? Because if you're going to be sick then you need to get out of my lake."

"Your lake?"

"There is something wrong with you," the otter replied curtly. "Do you not see you are in a lake?"

I looked over my shoulder and saw the vast expanse of water with scattered islands off in the distance and remained profoundly confused. How was this happening? Or better yet, why was this happening? Where in the hell was I?

It took a few minutes before I could gather myself, but as I looked around I realized I was standing on the edge of the muddy bank with tall trees in the distance. I could see the sun rising over the water just as the sky glistened a beautiful rose gold with ombre shades of purple and blue—just like in my dream. But this wasn't my dream or was it?

I can openly admit I have been mentally lost for months, but now as I sit here with an irate otter yelling at me, the idea of lost took on a whole new meaning. I'm talking, *I've hit my head too hard and now I live in the land of delirium,* kind of lost. The otter kept talking, but I couldn't hear what he was saying. I just watched as he feverishly waved his arms around as if to get me to respond. What was he trying to tell me? What was it that he wanted me to do as he pointed towards the shoreline?

I closed my eyes again, hoping sanity would bring me back to the real world, instead my mind drifted back to the day my world changed. The day my life had gone from being structured and predictable, to something I couldn't comprehend or recognize. I woke up the same as I had done every day for years and followed my regular routine…shower, makeup, hair, breakfast. My life, for all intents and purposes, was one big monotonous chord. That's not how I intended it to be, though. I had big plans. Plans so big that I was willing to leave the place and the people who mattered most to me in this world for a shot at bringing those *big* plans to fruition. I, like so many others, believed I was destined to be so much more. I failed to realize, though, that life was—correction, *IS* about more than whether or not you have the best job, best apartment, trendiest clothes, most likes on social media. It's about so much more, but I gave up that version of happy to pursue my dreams and now those dreams have brought me here. Failure.

I was pulled out of my recount when a sharp object dug into my ribcage. "Ow!" I exclaimed. My hand went for the spot, and when I pulled it back it was covered in blood. *Shit, this is not a dream.*

"Hello. Hello," two voices spoke in succession.

"She is hurt."

"Yes, she is."

"Will you heal her or shall I?"

"I think you should heal her, sister, since I never meant to hurt her to begin with. Fix her before I am forced to look away."

"Yes, dear sister. I shall fix her."

A warm sensation radiated from the wound, and I looked up at the two identical doll like females standing before me. Glancing down, I saw the wound had not only been healed, but the blood was gone too, washed away as if it never happened.

"Can someone please explain to me what the hell is going on?" I quipped.

"Language. That is a violation, and in front of the queens no less," the otter said as he shook his fist at me. "You'll do best to get up and bow if you know what is good for you."

"There is."

"No need."

"For that, Winston."

"We shall forgive."

"The transgression this time."

My eyes darted between them as they spoke back-to-back in incomplete sentences. I didn't know what to think or do. It was annoying and eerily disturbing at the same time, but honestly, a talking otter was pointing out my misbehavior, so who was I to say what was maddening at this point? I sat up slowly and made my way out of the water. My teeth had started to chatter, and I really wanted to understand what was going on. Where was I?

I stood before the two ethereal beings, dressed identically in all pink, including their hair and the rose gold crowns dripping in glinting crystals that adorned their heads. The only thing about them that wasn't bathed in a carnation hue was their turquoise colored eyes and pale peach skin.

"Um, I didn't mean to, ugh, yeah," I stammered as I tried to make myself presentable in spite of the circumstances. Water was dripping down my jeans, and the fabric of my top was clinging to my chest as if it were glued onto me, but I needed answers, and I was convinced these *people* were the only ones able to give them to me. "Can you please tell me where I am?"

"You are in Sacrife, of course."

"Where did you think you were, child?"

"Um, I wasn't sure."

"You use that word a lot, what does it mean?" the uptight otter snapped.

I closed my eyes and shook my head. "It's a bad habit. *Um* is a word used when someone is trying to come up with other words to say."

"You really should use correct language, but then again, you've been improper since you arrived."

"You are very rude," I fired back.

The twin queens chuckled in unison and then spoke together. "He doesn't know how to be any other way." They wiggled their fingers haphazardly in the air before calling Winston over to them. As they bent down and whispered something into his ear, he listened for a moment but then pulled back in shock. He tried to protest, but they denied him a rebuttal. Instead, he scurried off without another word or glance in my direction.

The queens shifted their attention to me and stared for several moments before snapping their fingers. Instantly, I was wearing dry clothes but not *my* clothes. My outfit had been replaced with a white silky blouse, tight black pants, and knee-high lace up boots. I looked up at the queens who seemed pleased with themselves, but the one on the right tilted her head slightly as if she wanted to change one more thing about me. She smiled and snapped her fingers again. I watched in awe as the bottom of my long hair started to change. The pale pink color climbed up-and-up, replacing the dirty blonde. Now my hair looked exactly like theirs. I was now a third to their duo.

"Yes."

"Perfect."

"She is flawless now."

I started to ask what was wrong with me before, but really, what was the point? This was all some effed-up dream I was having, and I was going to either wake up or be forced to accept that I was dead and this was either heaven or hell, depending on how I looked at it.

Winston had made his way back to where we were standing, but he wasn't alone. There beside him was a smaller but equally stodgy otter. However, this one was dressed in tan knickers, a bow tie, *Harry Potter* spectacles, and had a quiver draped over his small frame.

"Pleased to be at your service again," he said as he bowed to the queens.

What was with the talking otters? *God, I really wish I would wake up.*

Chapter Two

"Your majesties." Winston bowed too. "My son, as you requested."

The flowers rustled behind where the second otter stood. "Such a pleasure to see you again, Oliver," the one queen said.

"Indeed, a pleasure. Our best guide is now at your service," the second queen paused as she turned towards me. "We do not know your name, child."

"No we do not. What name are you called?"

I swallowed hard and looked around as everyone stared at me intently. It's not as if what they asked was difficult, but it's just that I still couldn't believe I was stuck in this ridiculous delusion.

"She's broken again," Winston gripped.

I threw him a look and turned to face the queens. "I'm not broken. Not really," I sighed. "My name is Novaleigh. Novaleigh Darrow."

"What a"

"beautiful"

"name."

Again, the queens spoke in broken sentences, but the reason remained unknown. Sometimes they carried out complete thoughts, while others were choppy and oddly child-like.

"Creative."

"Outgoing."

"Uncertainty."

"The trinity surrounds her."

"Such blessings to be counted in threes."

"I don't understand. What does that mean? Where am I? And why is this all happening?" I asked as I ran my fingers through my hair. "I appreciate your kindness and all, but what is going on?"

"Chosen."

"The aura surrounding you declares it."

"The color of your locks will now afford you safekeeping, not only for the fact that pink is our royal creed, but because you yourself share the gift."

"The gift?" I stammered. "What gift?"

"Clairaudience."

"Have you not already heard voices speaking to you?"

I stared at the queens blankly.

"The voice who told you to breathe?" the one queen said with a slight tilt of her head. "When you were drowning?"

Tears welled in my eyes. "Yes, I remember. I thought it was my own voice begging me to save myself."

"No."

"You are here because you have something to learn."

"The only way for you to return is to accept."

"To move forward."

"To carry the weight of the burden you bear."

"The pink is to remind you of the place you must get back to."

"For the place you are in now is bleak."

"Let it not go from black to white, for then all will be lost."

Now, tears were streaming down my face. How could they know I carried a burden and needed to heal? This was insane. I had officially lost my mind. Total "white jacket, white room" moment. All I needed now was a bouncy floor beneath my feet and it would all be over.

"Novaleigh."

"Oliver will be your guide. He will show you the way."

"Trust and faith have left you."

"He will help guide you back to them."

"Blessings to you on your journey.

"For now we must go."

"But..." I tried to protest, but in a flash they were gone.

I stood there crying for a few moments before I realized Winston and Oliver were still with me. I abruptly swiped my eyes and turned to look at them.

"Oliver was it?" The otter gave a clipped nod. "Where to first?"

Oliver looked over at Winston then back at me. "I am to guide you, but you are to choose the path."

I shook my head and whispered, "Of course I am." I looked around and tried to decide the best route to take. I hadn't noticed it before, but there seemed to be sections or quadrants with paths running along each one. I watched as a handful of autumn hued leaves rustled past my feet and towards a forest of deciduous trees in varying stages of change.

To the left of that was a path covered in a blanket of white, untouched and unsullied; just looking at it sent a chill up my spine. The other two paths were bathed in sunlight with brightly hued flowers rustling as a breeze kissed their leaves.

"Might I suggest something?" Winston offered, his tone more subdued and less critical than it had previously been. "Choose the direction your heart is pulling you towards. That will be the one you are meant to begin with."

My hands were shaky, and I could feel myself wanting to crawl into a ball and cry until I was able to snap out of this— whatever this was—but I knew that wasn't going to happen. I was going to have to see this through if I wanted my sanity to return. Onward and upward.

"I'd like to go that way," I said as I pointed towards the leafless trees in the distance.

Chapter Three

Oliver and I had walked for what seemed like miles, and yet we still had not reached the clearing where I'd hope to start my journey. When I chose the destination, it didn't look much more than a block away, and yet as my legs began to burn from the descent down the hill, I realized it wasn't as close as I thought.

"How far away is this place?"

"Cadent? Roughly a half days journey, why?"

"Really? It didn't seem that far away."

"Illusory, mistress. All things here in Sacrife are. Always changing and growing. It is a way for us to remain safe from the things that threaten to destroy us."

"Destroy you? I don't understand. This place is perfect and free. What could possibly destroy what the queens rule over?" I asked as if any of this was making sense. I wanted so desperately to wake from this dream/nightmare, but until I did, I assumed it was best to play along. Follow it through to its end, even if the end is the finale. *Acceptance.*

"As in all life, there must be balance. Light to dark. Good to bad. Earth to Sky. You get my point. Sacrife is no different, Novaleigh. So far, you've only encountered things associated with the light, but before you know it we will run into the others, the tricksters. You will need to take heed and not be drawn into their deceptions, understand?" Oliver said in a stern but soft tone.

"Sure. I guess."

"It will make sense when you encounter something that makes you recall our present conversation," Oliver said as he looked towards the path we were on.

"Are you always so serious? Your father was, and I guess that is where you learned it from, but do you ever have a moment of frivolity?"

Oliver turned and stared at me with a look of abject horror. "Frivolity? There is no room for silliness when you are a guardian. I take my job very seriously. If I don't—well, things can happen."

"Like what, Ollie?"

Oliver's eyes grew wide. "Excuse me, but my name is Oliver Franklin Hamilton. Do not address me so informally if you expect me to respond."

I pursed my lips together to stifle the laugh threatening to claim me. It's amazing what the unconscious mind conjures when it's in a state of trauma. An otter in clothing telling me to be formal and proper. *Yeah, okay.*

Oliver stopped abruptly and stared up at me. "This is no joke. You are here for a reason. You have something to learn, and I am to be your guide and keep you safe as you travel your chosen path, but by no means am I not to be taken seriously. Do we understand one another, Ms. Darrow?"

I swallowed hard. "Yes, Mr. Hamilton. Serious it is." I moved to go around him but stopped short before continuing on. "On one condition."

"Which is?" Oliver snapped.

"You call me Novi. It's what my friends call me."

His shoulders dropped and he relaxed. "I can agree to those terms," Oliver said as he adjusted his quiver. "But only if you continue to call me Oliver. Mr. Hamilton sounds as though my father is nearby and well, I'm not as stern as he is." He grinned.

We walked a bit more before either of us spoke again. This time, however, the conversation was more casual. We talked about the weather here and why sometimes a chill ran in the air despite the fact that there were rows and rows of peonies and marigolds in full bloom. Oliver explained that here, the seasons crossed one another based on the queens' whims.

"So this place we are headed, Cadent. Isn't that what you called it? Why are the trees there bare and look dead when everything else seems so vibrant and alive?"

Oliver gave me a sidelong glance before he spoke. "Cadent is its name. It means autumn or harvest. It most clearly is a season of change. Those who dwell there are in the in-between. If you linger too long, you can become trapped," he said with a slight tick in his jaw. "I was going to tell you this when we arrived—just before we entered, but since you are asking now, I felt I should explain."

I nodded. "Okay. Anything else I need to know or prepare for?"

He nodded. "You may see people or things that you want to help, but it is imperative that you only observe. They are on their path, and it is not for you or I to interfere or alter. Understand?"

"Yes."

Oliver pulled a looking glass out of the satchel attached to his belt and stared off into the distance. "I think this is a good place to stop and rest. We can make Cadent in two hours if we continue at the pace we've been going. I'm hungry, are you?"

I hadn't actually thought about it, but now that Oliver mentioned it, I was a little hungry. "I could eat, but the question is, what are we going to eat? It's not like there is a restaurant nearby."

"A what?"

I shook my head. "Never mind."

"Over here looks like a good place," Oliver said as he pointed to a clearing with two tree stumps covered in moss.

I watched as he pulled a cord from under his shirt. A cord carrying a large clear crystal wrapped in some kind of vine. He held it towards the sun and a dozen or so rays of light beamed towards the clearing. Within seconds, the stumps became stools and a round table appeared covered in bowls and goblets, all on glinting display. He turned to look at me. "What do you think?"

My mouth hung agape. What was I supposed to say? "How did you do that?"

Oliver grinned. "Magic of course. What else would it be?"

He didn't wait for me to respond, instead he trotted off towards the table and lifted the covers to reveal the fruits in one bowl and a variety of nuts in the other. As he reached for one, he turned to look at me. "I don't think you'll like these, but I'll be happy to share," he said as he lifted the lid on the last container. Inside was a variety of seafood—clams, mussels, sea urchins, snails, and a few small fish, eyes and all.

I scrunched my nose. "I think I'm good. That is all you, my friend."

He gave a broad smile and dished out a hearty portion for himself. "I didn't know your specific taste, so I started with something simple. Would you prefer something besides the fruits and nuts?"

"Maybe some cheese? I really love apples, cheese, and walnuts."

Oliver nodded, and with a few choice words as he held up the crystal, a plate full of cheese arrived on my side of the table.

"Thank you," I said as I took the seat opposite him. It wasn't much really, but it was perfect. The food was wonderful, and before I could even request it, Oliver called out for drinks and the most delicious concoction appeared before us. It looked like a thick dark wine, but it tasted like a modified version of a piña colada. Fresh pineapples, creamy coconut, and dark sweet cherries, all smoothly blended but without any alcohol. I was literally in love with each sip and drank at least three goblets full by the time the meal had ended.

"For having arrived out of thin air, this meal was divine, Oliver," I said with a grin.

Oliver puffed out his chest and tucked his bound crystal into his satchel. "It was nothing, honest."

"Well, it was most appreciated. I now have the energy to carry on to Cadent."

"We will be there before sundown and should have enough time to find shelter before the dark settles in."

I nodded and followed as Oliver made his way back onto the path. The closer we got to Cadent, the more vivid the scenery became. The sky was a brilliant mix of orange and gold, while the spindly trees created an eerie foreground. As we got closer, Oliver stopped.

"What is it?"

"I need to make you aware of this place and the things you may encounter," Oliver said as he pulled a large bag out of his satchel.

"How big is that bag? You certainly have a lot in it."

He shook his head in disregard. "It carries all I need it to carry, Novi. Things we may need on our journey. I couldn't pack everything, but I planned for the obvious of course."

"Of course." I smiled. "So what is it you need to tell me about?" Just as I spoke, a giddy sound of laughter echoed through the trees. "What was that?"

Oliver adjusted his glasses and reached into the pouch he was carrying. "That was part of what I needed to tell you about." He pulled out a handful of purple flower buds and then the crystal he used earlier to make our meal appear. "I'll explain in a moment. Right now I need to ready myself for their arrival."

"Whose arrival?" Another round of high pitched laughter rang out, but this time it was accompanied by the rustling of the autumn hued maple leaves scattering all around. The leaves danced as a gentle breeze blew. Oliver worked faster to call forth whatever he needed before the leaves settled back onto the ground again. In one hand Oliver held the buds and in the other a small glass pitcher of what looked like milk. "What is that for?" I snapped.

Oliver didn't answer, instead he took a knee and bowed his head. "Do as I do, and I'll explain later," he whispered.

I, too, bent down and bowed towards the entrance to Cadent, waiting and wondering why all of this was necessary. Again, wondering why this dream I was stuck in was so incredibly unusual. I sighed and waited. A heartbeat later my answer arrived.

"You wish to enter?" A deep voice spoke only a few feet away.

"We do," Oliver said as he held out the offerings.

"You may rise, Sir Hamilton."

Oliver stood, and the tension I had in my shoulders eased. While this whole situation was peculiar, I found myself full of anxiety. Who was this person that Oliver had to bow to, I wondered? When I looked up I saw nothing. Oliver cleared his throat and flicked his head towards the ground. There before us was a tiny man with thorny wings covered in a gossamer leaf. I stared in disbelief as the overly small creature sheathed his sword.

"Are you going to introduce me to your guest, Sir Hamilton?"

Oliver stammered a bit, then recovered. "This is Miss Novaleigh Darrow. She is an honorary guest of the queens as you can see by her hair."

"Pleased to meet you, Miss Darrow. It's an honor to have you here in Cadent," he said with a tilt of his head.

"And you are?" I replied.

"Mabellio. Warrior leader of the Autumn Fae and direct council to Golar the Golden Queen."

I looked over at Oliver, hoping to gather some sort of insight, but he was just standing there, looking out at the thirty some odd little fairies who had appeared out of nowhere and were now bowing before me. I didn't know what to say or do, so instead I smiled.

"We request permission to travel through your land," Oliver asked as he put his hand in his pocket and pulled out a nugget of silver. "We'd like to offer payment in advance if you will accept us."

Mabellio stepped forward to accept the chunk of silver. "Golar will be pleased. Thank you for the offering. You may enter, but be forewarned that there are travelers among us who may be less than desirable. Some have been trapped, while others still roam. We shall catch them soon enough, and our watchers will keep an eye out as you journey on."

"Your kindness is appreciated. We will take heed of your warning," Oliver replied.

"Safe travels my friend," Mabellio said as he pulled out a handful of dirt and blew it into the air. A smoky cloud wafted into the sky and illuminated an entrance that was previously hidden. "You may enter."

Oliver reached for my hand and together we entered Cadent.

"I'll explain when we find shelter. Until then just follow me."

I sighed and followed.

Chapter Four

We didn't have to go far before we reached our intended destination. I was tired, hungry, and quite frankly over all the mysticism that was constantly surrounding me. Everywhere I turned, something was alive and moving about in a hurried yet calm fashion. Daily life for the creatures and things that lived in Cadent, I supposed, but until I could ask Oliver, I was forced to assume, and we all know what assuming does for you.

"It's just up those stairs. Follow me," Oliver said as he walked towards an arched stone wall with steps running up the side. The whole thing looked as though it had, at one time or another, been part of a larger structure, but now looked as if it may fall down at any moment.

"Oliver," I snapped as I stopped short of the first step. "There is nothing at the top of this and even if there was, I doubt those stairs can hold my weight. This can't possibly be where we are going."

"But it is Novi, and it will hold your weight. Before this land became home to the Autumn Fae, it was a place where humans like yourself used to dwell. They built them. What is still standing will more than carry your size."

I huffed. "Maybe so then, but those stone steps still lead to nothing. It just drops off."

"Faith, Novi. Faith."

Oliver was halfway up the stairs to nowhere when he stopped to wave me on. With each step I took, the scenery changed behind it. The moss covered stone began to glint in the sun's setting glow, and lightening bugs began to brighten our way in the dusk. At the top, there was an arched wooden door with a copper handle and a sign that read *Welcome*.

"Where did that come from, Oliver?" I huffed.

He laughed and turned the handle. "Our respite for the night, mistress."

I ducked through the small doorway, expecting to have to crawl around on the inside. But as with everything else in this land, the height of the door was misleading. Instead of the tiny space I'd imagined, there was a multi-level home with quaint furnishings and golden lanterns that twinkled as candle flames danced within.

I turned to Oliver as he removed his quiver and bow, hanging them on the hook beside the door and asked, "Is everything in Cadent magical?"

"Everything in Sacrife is magical, Novi. Nothing is as it seems. You must remember this."

"Well, quite frankly, I'm still wondering when I am going to wake up from this insane dream. I know none of this is real," I said as I plopped down on a couch near the fireplace and closed my eyes.

Oliver laughed a full-on belly laugh as he made his way towards the kitchen. "This is no dream, Novi. Everything you are experiencing is real and until you accept that, you will not be able to go home."

"Yeah, okay. Sure. Twin queens, talking otters, Autumn Fae, houses suspended in midair. Yep, totally real. Got it."

Oliver shook his head. "Why are you here, Novaleigh?"

"I have no idea, Oliver. Why am I here?"

"You know the reason. You just choose not to accept it."

I opened one eye and stared at him. "No, I do not. One minute I was standing on the bridge by my grandparent's place, and then next I was here. Nothing more, nothing less."

"And what exactly lead to you being there?" Oliver jibed.

I sat there in silence, thinking about his question. What had brought me so close to the water's edge? How did I get here? I know I wasn't pushed, I was alone. I also know I didn't *jump*. Could I have slipped? Moments passed as I recounted all the events that led me back to Scotland in the first place. I had been in New York, working at my job, until the day I decided I needed and wanted more. I thought that was what we were supposed to do as humans, follow a path but stray a bit so we could grow. I swear, that was all I was trying to do, but everything went wrong—everything.

Two and a half months had passed since I enthusiastically decided to give my boss an ultimatum and ended up without a job. And exactly four weeks and three days since I found my jackass boyfriend banging his secretary. The final nail in the coffin, though, was the day I realized that no matter what I did to pursue other employment, I'd never work in New York again. Mr. Kline had successfully blackballed me with every potential employer. I was finished.

"Are you hungry? I was going to fix us something to eat. We have a long day's journey tomorrow, and we'll need our strength," Oliver asked, interrupting my little jaunt down memory lane.

I sat up and nodded. "Yes, please."

"So have you figured out why you are here?"

"I lost my job and my boyfriend cheated on me, but I hardly think those things are reasons to end up in a friggin' magical wonderland, do you?" I asked, not really expecting an answer.

"Again. That is not why you are here. Look deeper."

"Ugh," I sighed as I flopped back onto the couch.

Oliver went back to what he was doing, and I was left to dwell on my own thoughts. I grew up in a small town just outside of New York. My parents were teachers and we lived a quaint, peaceful life. We spent summers at my dad's parents in Scotland and I loved it there too. It wasn't until my parents separated that my mom decided to move us to Scotland permanently. We lived in the guest house on my grandparents' property while my mom went back to school to get her Master's degree. After graduation, she accepted a teaching position at the University of Glasgow, but I wanted to move back to New York and work for one of the big publishing houses instead of following her. It had always been my dream, for as long as I could remember. I even had a map with strings and pins over my bed of all the places in the city I would visit once I was an official resident again. I was drunk with the idea.

It's not that I didn't love Scotland. I did. I wanted to live fast paced, though, in the city that didn't sleep, not in a town that rolled up the sidewalks before 10pm. I had a plan, and I wasn't going to be swayed from it for anything or anyone.

My heart clenched. Gavin had been the one thing that gave me pause, but we were young and stupid. What were we gonna do, stay on the path we were on which had me married at twenty-two and most likely a mother by twenty-five? I didn't think so. My heart clenched again. I loved Gavin, and he was the hardest thing I had to give up when I made my choice, but I had to do it for me. *Selfish.* I broke his heart when I left, but he wasn't the only one. My mom and grandparents had hoped for more too, and I let them all down. The joke was on me, though, because I gave them all up just to end up with nothing. I lost more than just a lousy boyfriend and a shitty boss too. My pappa had a stroke one spring, and I hadn't been there for my nanna after he passed. I couldn't get the time off and so when she needed me the most, I wasn't there. Mom drove the distance from Glasgow to Isle of Skye weekly to help out, and they had help from Gavin and his dad, but me, nope, I wasn't available. I was living my *dream*.

Tears started to well in my eyes as thoughts of all the things I should have been there for and the reasons why I wasn't hit me like a tidal wave. I didn't have time to wallow in it, though, because Oliver walked over and handed me a plate of corned beef and cabbage with a side of steaming carrots and potatoes. And if that wasn't good enough, he had two slices of freshly baked soda bread with butter on the plate as well.

"How did you know this was my favorite?" I asked.

Oliver shrugged. "I didn't. I made my favorite and hoped you'd like it."

I started slow at first, savoring every bite, but then I couldn't help myself. I mashed the potatoes and carrots and turned the whole meal into a makeshift hash. It was the way I used to eat it as a kid when Nanna used to make it.

When I took the last bite, and my plate was spotless, I turned to Oliver who was happily sated as well. "You know, if this guardian gig doesn't continue to work out, maybe you should consider a career as a chef."

We both chuckled and then sighed happily at our full bellies.

Neither of us said anything for a bit. Instead we both just sat in silence and enjoyed the peace of the moment. Eventually, Oliver moved, grabbing up our plates and walking into the kitchen.

"Hey, let me do the dishes. It's the least I can do."

"I'll meet you halfway," he said as he grabbed a dishtowel out of the cupboard. "I'll dry."

I grinned. "Deal."

We started on the plates, but by the time we got to the pots and pans, Oliver started asking me questions again. "Did you learn anything while I was cooking?"

I gave him a downward glance. "No."

"Have you always been so stubborn?" he asked as he took the pan out of my hand to dry.

"What is that supposed to mean?"

"It means that you must like all this confusion and being here in Sacrife, otherwise you'd try harder to uncover the root of your pain."

I dropped the pot I was washing. "How do you know I'm in pain?"

"Because the only reason your kind end up in Sacrife is from some sort of pain, and it's usually self-inflicted. I was given to you as a gift by the queens because they said you were special, that your arrival had been prophesied. You were to come here, and I am to get you home."

"What?!"

"Look, I can understand your frustration, but if we work together we can get you home."

My shoulders dropped. "I'm not special. Far from it. Why me? Why here?"

"That I don't know, Novi. The instructions I was given was to take you wherever you want to go and to keep you safe."

"So let me understand this...anyone, other than me, does not get a welcome wagon from the queens and is now currently roaming around Sacrife struggling to find their way without someone like yourself to guide them?"

Oliver took off his glasses, wiped them on his shirt and put them back on. "Yes. That is what I am saying. Some of your kind die here, Novi, and some are trapped in limbo. There is, however, the rare individual that manages to find their way out on their own, but that usually never happens without a specific motivation."

"Everything is just as screwed up here as it was at home. This place has no answers. I'm not going to find anything here."

Oliver reached up for my hand and led me back into the living room area. "Can we try something?"

I rolled my eyes. "Do I really have a choice?"

"You always have a choice, Novi," Oliver said as he pointed towards the chair next to the couch. "Sit. I know a way for you to open your mind to the places you keep hidden."

"Oliver, I told you. I had normal problems stemming from poor choices. I'll get past it. The world will move on. *I will move on.*"

"Humor me?" Oliver asked as he walked over to his satchel and pulled out a vibrant blue stone. "Lay your head back on the cushion and get comfortable."

"You are a very odd otter, Oliver."

He laughed and then placed the stone on my forehead. "Close your eyes."

"Care to explain?" I asked.

"No. The stone will begin to work soon enough."

"What is this...thing?"

"It's a lapis lazuli and it will help us, I mean you, get to the source of what's bothering you. Once we do that, then I can better guide you on this journey. So close your eyes, and let's begin."

I sighed and did as he asked. *I really don't want to do this, but then again, I really don't want to spend the rest of my days trapped in this whacked out dream and living in limbo either. Maybe I fell and hit my head and am in a coma. Yeah, that seems logical.*

"Quiet your mind, Novaleigh. The stone cannot work if you continue to be resistant to it," Oliver advised.

"But I didn't say a word. How did you know?"

"Shhhhh," he whispered.

Chapter Five

Whatever this lapis lazuli was, it began to work–or at least I thought it was doing something—almost immediately. It had turned ice cold then warmed slightly until it was comfortably cool against my skin. Visions of water began to rush through my mind, and I drifted into a deep sleep, lulled by the gentle waves of energy flowing through me. Now that I was in a calm state, I was halted, unsure of what I was supposed to do next. I heard a muffled voice echo in my mind but couldn't identify who it was. The voice grew closer but remained muted.

"What? I can't hear you. What are you saying?"

"Follow the water. Follow the light."

"I don't understand. Follow the what?"

"Water, light, flame, purify."

"That makes no sense."

"Breathe."

I took a deep breath and was transported to a memory.

Susan: Are you seriously going to follow through with this?

I picked up my phone and texted back.

Novi: Yep! If I don't I'll be lost forever.

Susan: Drama queen.

Novi: LOL. See you at work.

I left my house and drove to the office still debating my plan, but like I told Susan, if I didn't do this now, I never would. I don't want to be stuck in a dead-end job with nothing to claim as an adventure under my belt. There will always be other jobs. Besides, it's not as if I don't deserve this. I work my ass off for Mr. Kline, and he knows I cannot be replaced, yet he still continues to screw me on the bonuses and advances.

I'm going on vacation to visit my mom next week, hell or high water. Mr. Kline can either give me the time off, or I'll quit.

My forehead warmed and my mind flashed forward.

"Hi, this is Novaleigh Darrow. May I speak with Allison Simmons?"

"Please hold."

"Hey, Novi. How are you?"

"I'm good, but I wanted to give a heads up. You've always been more than just a client, and I couldn't in good faith just leave you in the dark."

"Okay, you're freaking me out. What's going on?"

"I gave Mr. Kline a chance to prove he was a decent human being today, but he failed miserably. I gave him my notice."

"Are you kidding me? What asshole move did he pull now?"

"I asked for two weeks vacation." I laughed.

"Mr. Kline is such a greedy bastard. He'll never find anyone to replace you. He's a moron."

"Yeah, I know, but he doesn't see it that way."

"When is your last day?" Allison sighed.

"Today. Mr. Kline said if I wasn't willing to play ball the way he wanted it played, then I could leave. I'm actually calling you from the Starbucks down the street from your office."

"Don't move. I'll be there in five."

Allison walked in the door and made her way to the counter to order her usual—venti green tea latte, before making a beeline to where I was sitting by the window.

"All right, I have a plan," Allison said as she dropped her bags on the table.

I laughed. "You always do."

My body shivered, and I felt like I was going to throw up. I took another deep breath and tried to focus again. A few moments and a few more waves of nausea hit me before I was able to regain my internal balance. Then my mind flashed again.

I'm a confidant young woman and skilled at my job, but Mr. Kline was a stodgy old man who liked to bark simply for the fun of it. I had worked tirelessly for that man for two years. Two years of out-working the other assistants and yet every time they were the ones to get the bonuses. They were the ones to get time off and special consideration when it came to advancement. Mr. Kline always chose everyone else above me, and I'd finally had enough. In fact, the months prior to this whole ordeal had been hellacious. I decided to ask for some time off and a raise for all my efforts. I'd added three new clients to our publishing house's roster in the last three weeks, so again, I didn't think asking for few days off for myself was anything exorbitant. Unfortunately, what I didn't know was that the other three assistants had beaten me to the punch and already put in for their days off.

Mr. Kline was a stickler for unwavering dedication and didn't feel vacation time was necessary, but since the law required it, he had to comply. By the time I'd worked up the nerve to ask, Mr. Kline was thoroughly irritated.

And then there had been Ethan, my jackass of a boyfriend, and the skank from his office. Since I'd lost my job I admit that I'd been a bit difficult to be around, but I was trying to make amends and decided to surprise Ethan with dinner at the office. He'd been working late a lot, but

I thought that is what junior associates did to try and make partner. Boy, how wrong I was. Ethan was just screwing his way through his office instead. I should've been shocked or angry, but I was neither. When I walked in and saw the two of them going at it, I just stood there and watched for a second before I dropped the food containers drawing their attention to me. Liza choked out a scream and Ethan proceeded to make excuses.

"Wait Novaleigh! It's not what you think!"

"Not what I think? No, you're right. It looked like the two of you were knitting." I grabbed the umbrella in the stand next to the door and chucked it at him. "Fuck off, Ethan. We're done."

"But wait. I can explain."

"No need. I know all I need to know."

He tried to chase after me but tripped over the pants around his ankles. It would've been humorous if the truth of what I'd just witnessed hadn't hit me so hard. I'd wasted a year and a half with a man who lacked the ability to be faithful and spent two years busting my ass for another man who couldn't see my worth. Those two events had been the beginning of my downward spiral. Normally, I'm a strong person, difficult to break, but with them both happening back to back, it felt as though the universe was rising up against me.

Everything happens in threes, my nanna always used to say. I spent the next few weeks waiting for the third thing to knock me on my ass so I could finally pick myself up, but what do they say when you're in the midst of hell? That there is something better ahead? I get the concept, but the idea is completely screwed up when all you want to do is rage and eat pints and pints of ice cream to drown the sorrow and self-pity.

I coughed and my eyes flew open. I stared at Oliver who was staring back at me with concern.

"Are you okay?" he asked.

"What was that? It's like I was reliving everything."

"Lapis lazuli is a powerful crystal with amazing healing properties. I chose it for you so you can tap into the thoughts you need to unblock."

I sat up and got dizzy. "Whoa."

"I think that is enough for tonight. We can try again tomorrow. You probably should just go to bed now."

"Okay." I nodded. "Is here on the couch all right?"

"Actually there is a room at the top of the stairs waiting for you. Pillows, blankets, and anything you might need."

"Wow. Thank you, again. I know I keep saying that, but that's truly how I feel. Thank you for taking care of me, Oliver."

"It's no bother, Novi."

I stood and headed for the stairs but stopped and turned back to Oliver. "Sorry I gave you and your dad such a hard time when I first arrived. It was all a lot to take in, you know?"

He grinned. "I do. Sleep well."

"You too, Oliver."

Chapter Six

Dawn arrived before I knew it, and Oliver and I were out the door. I had no idea where we were going, but we certainly seemed to be in a hurry to get there.

"Why the rush?" I asked as we made our way down the stone steps.

"We have to meet with Golar, the Autumn Fae Queen, by a quarter till. We have to hurry. We slept in when we should have been on our way a half hour ago," Oliver said as he tossed a handful of a chalky substance into the air near the base of the steps. In an instant, the cottage we were staying in vanished.

"Why do we have to meet the queen?" I asked as we continued to hurry down the leaf littered path.

"It is customary when you visit her land to join her in a feast. We arrived too late yesterday. She is an early riser and prefers to celebrate early. Hence, the rushing," he said as he picked up his pace. "She abhors late. I don't want to be late."

I walked faster because the panic in his voice demanded it. We had been walking through a picturesque version of fall. I mean, snap a photo of your ideal November day and you were where we were, but as we rounded the bend, the landscape changed. The trees were as high as the sky with their bark appearing almost black and the leaves were varying shades of burgundy and red. It was stunning but alarming. I'd never seen this much vibrancy, and it was breathtaking.

"Is this where we're going?" I asked.

"Yes. Just down that path and we'll have arrived," Oliver said as he pulled out his watch, "and on time as well." He grinned.

The wood bridge creaked as I crossed, but it held my weight just like the stairs. *Magic again, I suppose.* Oliver reached the end of the path and came to a halt. There was nothing in front of him, yet he stopped and pulled out something from within his satchel.

"Again, I have to ask...how much stuff do you have in that bag, Oliver? It's like a damn clown car." I laughed.

He shook his head and turned back to what he was doing. "What is a clown car?"

"Nothing. Never mind. Why have you stopped?"

"There is a wall here. I need to ask for permission..." his words trailed off as I slid up next to him, trying to see the wall he was speaking of.

"Is it invisible, or am I just missing it?"

He shook his head. "The fairy realm is hidden from view. You can only see their home if they want you to."

I sat silent and listened to him speak another language as he swung a gold necklace in the shape of a tree in a circular motion. "What is that?"

"A replica of their sacred thorn tree. Golar will appreciate it," Oliver stated confidently between his chanting.

"How do you know this queen? You seemed on friendly terms with the fae we met last night. What was his name again?"

"Mabellio," Oliver blurted.

"Got it. Mabellio and Golar. I'm good with names. I won't embarrass you," I said as I stood still.

The invisible wall became fluid and the sound of gleeful singing filled the air. Oliver motioned for me to follow him. I stepped through the wall and was welcomed by a hundred or so tiny fae. Some of them were flying overhead, while others dangled from the leaves on the trees above. They were calling out and saying blessed greetings as Oliver and I continued to walk towards a large glowing tree. The tree was massive, at least fifty feet tall and was covered in little glinting lights that shimmered on the tips of the branches. It was magnificent.

Mabellio held up his hand and asked that we wait a moment. "The queen will be along momentarily. Can we get you something to drink?" he asked.

"Pear juice would be lovely, thank you," Oliver replied.

Mabellio looked at me. I nodded quickly. "That sounds wonderful, thank you."

A handful of fairies dressed in dark shades of green and gold gowns landed on my shoulder and began playing with my hair.

"So pretty," one exclaimed.

"Colorful."

"Soft," a third called out and she ran her fingers through the strands. "We like to comb our hair, do you?"

I smiled. "Well, yes, sometimes."

"Sometimes," she said curiously. "Do you not care for it every day?"

"I wash and dry it, but I've never really been big on styling it if that's what you mean."

"Oh dear," the three cried out and pulled jewel encrusted combs from hidden pockets within their dresses. "We'll fix you," they sang as they began to stroke my hair.

I glanced over at Oliver who just gave me a terse smile. He wasn't going to be any help. I'm not sure how much time passed before Golar emerged from a door within the tree but one thing was for sure, I had now been bedazzled. Leaves and feathers had been woven into my hair, thanks to the three fae stylists. I had sat to get comfortable while they played with my locks, but now that their queen arrived, they all rose and bowed. I followed suit, of course.

There wasn't any pomp and circumstance as I assumed there would be, instead, Golar waved at the gathered crowd and walked towards Oliver and me.

"It is wonderful to see you again, Oliver," the queen said with a hint of glee in her voice.

I'm not sure what I expected to see, but she was far from any assumptions I'd made. Golar could not have been more than six inches tall and was dressed in a lavishly rich chocolate brown gown. It was hard to see, but as she moved, the thread on her dress cast hues of orange and gold. I watched intently as she and Oliver carried on their pleasantries. Her hair was halfway down her back and was a shimmer of amber and blonde. Her skin was pale, almost transparent in the sun, and her voice sounded like pure joy. She was captivating.

The small queen turned her attention to me and flew on her gossamer wings until we were almost face to face. "And you must be, Novaleigh."

"I am," I replied a little too breathy and blew the queen backwards a bit. "Oh my gosh, I am so sorry!"

The queen giggled and adjusted her dress and hair as she flew back towards me. "I don't see many your size. I shall make a concession to make our visit more enjoyable." She turned to the other fae and said something I didn't understand, but it was clear she told them to move because they all scattered immediately. In a flash, the queen was now as tall as I was. "There," she said with a smile, "much better."

"I'm really so very sorry. I'm not used to meeting queens and you are my second—sorry, third in two days," I said with a slight curtsy.

"This is truly our honor. It is not often we meet favored children of Una and Uphren. Thank you for visiting our home."

I was dumbfounded. She was honored to meet me? Why on earth?

"I have to tell you, Golar, you are stunningly beautiful. You're almost hypnotic to look at and listen to."

She smiled and blushed before bowing in my direction. "Your compliments please me greatly. Are you hungry?" she asked Oliver and me.

We both nodded and followed she turned to move towards a large banquet table that had appeared out of nowhere. It was covered in greenery, flowers, and every color of leaf you could imagine. There were overflowing trays filled with decadent foods spanning the entire table. Whether this was a dream or not, it really rocked at this point. It felt like I was in the best fairytale that had never been told. And if that wasn't enough, the fae were turning into life-sized humans as they made their way to the table. I think even Oliver had grown from his usual three feet to almost five. *I really need to write this dream down when I wake up. It could totally be a bestseller. I could name it, 'You Can't Make This Shit Up'.*

We all sat, and a toast was raised to Oliver and I, and then another to the fae queen and her family. It was lovely, and lively. After we ate, we danced and sang, and then rested in a bed of burgundy leaves. In that moment, I didn't have a care in the world. Mabellio walked over to where I was laying and asked if I could join him, Golar, and Oliver in the tree. We needed to speak about my visit.

"Oh. Yes. Of course," I replied as I stumbled trying to get out of the pile of leaves. Mabellio reached down and pulled me up. He too, was beautiful in a masculine way. Like a perfectly chiseled Armani model. His hair was dark brown, almost black, and his eyes were a perfect blend of hazel-green and gold. "Thank you," I said as I dusted myself off.

"No problem." He pointed towards the tree in the middle of the field. "It's this way."

"Can I ask you something?"

He nodded.

"Are all of you this hypnotic?"

He laughed.

"I'm sorry, I really don't mean to stare. It's just that, well, yeah," I stammered.

"It's our fae essence. Usually it's less noticeable, but when we are this size, it is *amplified*, if you will."

"Oh." I sighed. "You make me feel drunk."

He laughed again. "That may be the fae wine you've been drinking."

"Really? Okay, whew." I shook my head. "I mean, you are gorgeous, but drunk off looks seemed a bit shallow."

"You are an amusing human, Miss Darrow."

"Please, call me Novaleigh."

He tilted his head in a slight bow then reached for the door handle on the outside of the tree. I was so busy stammering over Mabellio that I hadn't realized we had reached our destination. He held open the door and gestured with his hand toward the spiral staircase that wound into the roots of the tree. I used the vine handrail and took each hand-carved step slowly since I was feeling a bit woozy. By the time I reached the bottom step I was a tad out of breath.

"Let me get you some water. The air down here can feel a bit tight if you aren't used to it," Mabellio offered.

He was back in a flash with a leaf shaped like a glass filled with icy cold water. "You're too kind."

"Please sit."

I sat down in the chair he pointed to and sank into its softness. The chair was made of woven vines and what looked like a ginormous mushroom for a cushion.

"You guys have the best stuuuuuufffff," I slurred.

Chapter Seven

I'm not sure how long I was out, but when I woke, Oliver, Golar, and Mabellio were sitting in the chairs across from me, conversing as if I hadn't been passed out moments ago.

"I—I'm so sorry. I don't know what happened there. I'm so embarrassed."

"Don't be," Golar replied. "It looks as though you needed the rest and we've been enjoying Oliver's company in the meantime. How are you feeling?"

"Better. Thank you"

"So we have been talking about your journey, Novaleigh, and it seems that you chose to come to my home first. Why is that?" Golar asked with a soft smile.

My heart began to race and my throat felt as if it were closing in on itself with each breath I took. I didn't know why I'd chosen Cadent first, and I doubted my true answer of *"It looked interesting and this is a crazy whacked out dream so I just followed it"* was going to be a proper response. Instead, I sat there dumfounded at the question in general. The longer the three stared at me, the more uncomfortable I became. Inadvertently, I started shaking my head and then finally found my voice.

"I really don't know. I thought it was beautiful from the distance and my heart was drawn to it," I finally said.

"Exactly. Your heart was drawn to it," Golar replied.

"I'm not sure I understand. I don't think there was anything deep and meaningful to my choice."

"Not true. Your heart wants to heal, but your mind is stopping it. The trick is to get the two to meld in unison so you can find your true happiness."

I cleared my throat. Heart hammering, hands shaking. "Um, Oliver. Exactly what did you tell them?" I asked pointedly.

He raised his hands in the air. "I told them nothing, Novi I swear it."

"Then why did this lovely visit turn into ar interrogation/therapy session?"

"I didn't say anything," he paused. "You did."

"Excuse me?"

Mabellio looked away awkwardly, and Golar shifted in her seat. Had I spilled my guts in my drunken fairy stupor? *Oh God!* Oliver walked over to me and placed his paw on my shaky hands as tears spilled down my cheeks.

"It's okay. We know now how to help you," Oliver soothed.

"Please tell me what I said." More tears spilled. "Please."

"I'll say this, we know about Gavin."

"Oh my god," I cried. "What the hell is wrong with me?"

"Nothing," Golar consoled. "With love comes pain and the greater the love, the greater the pain. These are nothing more than obstacles on the long path to your destiny, Novaleigh. It is how you deal with them that defines them and you."

I shook my head feverishly, hoping that I'd shake myself awake and out of this torture. *Talk Novi. Get out how you feel and you can be free. Fuck all of that. I don't want to talk about this. I don't want Oliver and Golar's infinite wisdom. I don't want to have this conversation. What happened between Gavin and me is my personal burden to bear. I don't need it fixed. I don't want it fixed. I am fully aware of the choices I made and the consequences of my decisions. But this*

here and now, NO! I am not reliving my worst moments to satisfy some screwed up notion of coming clean to be free.

I stood up and headed for the stairs. "I need to go. Thank you for the hospitality, but I need to leave," I blurted before I took the first step. "And you." I pointed to Oliver. "I don't need a guide anymore either."

I ran up the stairs without another word. With each step I took, the voices shouting at me to come back grew further and further away. I pushed open the door and ran out into the darkness. *How long had I been out? We came here this morning.* I continued to run, following the twinkling lights that were floating in the trees above me. I didn't know what they were, and at this point, I didn't really care. I just wanted out.

The landscape changed from joyful to dismal. I must have left Golar's hidden home and was now back in the forest I was in last night. My heart was racing, but my feet continued to carry me away from Oliver and his truthsayers. I felt free, as the wind blew through my hair. *Maybe you could run yourself into oblivion and either die or wake up, either way, the outcome would create a conclusion. You're such a fool, Novaleigh,* I thought to myself.

I stopped running when the fall leaves ceased to crunch beneath my feet and the ground, instead, started to feel unsteady. I looked down and realized I was standing in mud which wasn't the worse part; as I glanced around to see where I was, I learned I wasn't alone.

There, before me, was a pond surrounded by large patches of tall grass and spindly trees that swayed gently with the cool breeze. In the middle of the water was a man hunched over, bound to two tree stumps. He was moaning and in pain. I could feel it from where I stood. I moved towards him but stopped when a deep voice spoke in the darkness.

"Do not touch him."

I stood motionless, waiting to see who it was. It didn't sound like Mabellio, but who else could it be? A slender male stepped out of the tree line and stood in the moonlight. I took in his features and let out a gasp. I didn't mean to, but the sight of him took me aback. His face was stark white and crackled like dried mud, while his eyes were crimson and his teeth were solid black.

"Who are you?" I dared to ask.

"The warden of this land and the keeper of those who dare to cross my path," he snarled. "And who might you be?"

"I'm just someone who seems to have taken a wrong turn," I replied hesitantly.

"Well, you must be someone important," he said as his eyes flashed to my hair.

"I was given favor by the twin queens, Una and Uphren, nothing more."

He smirked and tilted his head. "Liar."

"I'm not lying. I was given favor."

"Of that I am certain. It is the '*nothing more*' that I doubt."

I swallowed hard. I wondered how much leeway I would be afforded with the pink in my hair. Could I save the man bound in the water with my '*favor*'? "Why is this man bound?"

"Why do you care?"

"Because he looks like he is in pain, and I want to help him."

"You don't seem like someone who cares about people in pain. He should be of no concern to you."

I huffed. What an asshole, but then again he was a warden. What did I expect from him, puppies and kittens? I lifted my chin and steadied my shoulders. "I demand to check on this man and confirm that he's not been mistreated."

"You demand?" the frightening man replied as he continued to glare at me. "He has been mistreated but not by me. I am just here waiting for the one who hurt him to return. It is them whom I wish to find." He waved his arm the direction of the bound man. "Be my guest."

I stepped out of the muck I'd been sinking in and moved to the water's edge. Slowly, I trudged towards the man until I was close enough to touch him.

"Sir. Are you okay?"

Nothing. No reply. I touched the man's shoulder and he winced. What had happened to him? Why was he bound like this? "I'd like to help you. Can you look at me?" I waited. "Please?"

The man moved a bit, his arms twisting in the restraints. He struggled and groaned but finally lifted his head to look at me. I gasped and covered my mouth. *How? Why? This isn't happening!* were the thoughts that raced through my mind like lightning.

"Gavin?"

Chapter Eight

"Novi? Why are you here?"

"Why are *you* here?"

The warden growled and pulled something long and shiny out from underneath the cloak he was wearing. "I had a feeling it was you," he snarled.

"Me? What? I didn't hurt him. I just got here."

"His wounds have healed and new ones have been formed. You could easily be his original perpetrator. Step away from him and move to the shore."

I didn't move.

"Or you can die," he threatened.

Just then Oliver and Mabellio came running out of the bushes. "HALT!" Oliver bellowed. We both turned to his booming voice. He was rather loud for an otter. "You are still on Cadent land and you have no jurisdiction here. Leave by order of Golar and the twin queens."

The warden moved the large knife and Mabellio, who was still as tall as a human male, raised his spear in warning. The freaky figure turned back to me and flashed a venomous grin my way. "We'll meet again, I am certain of it. You and I have much to discuss," he said just before vanishing in a haze of putrid yellow dust.

"Who the hell was that, and what did I do to piss him off so bad?"

"I'll explain later. We must go. It is not safe here."

"You always say that, Oliver. I'll explain later and you never do."

"Yes, yes. That may very well be, but believe me when I say we MUST go!" Oliver hissed. "It's not safe out here in the open."

"But why?" I demanded even as Mabellio and Oliver tried to drag me out of the water.

Before they could answer, a shrill cry echoed through the forest. The three of us froze, unsure of the direction the sound came from. Mabellio pulled out his spear, while Oliver readied his bow.

"Now, Novaleigh. We have to go now!" Mabellio yelled.

"Fine, but I'm not leaving him here to die from whatever's in the forest," I said as I pointed to Gavin.

"We can't take him," Oliver replied as he stared down the length of the arrow.

"We have to, Oliver. It's Gavin."

Both Oliver and Mabellio snapped their heads in my direction.

"Gavin?"

I nodded. "And I'm not leaving without him."

Mabellio and Oliver exchanged glances then Mabellio moved to help Gavin out of the restraints. I took the other side and helped to steady Gavin when he fell forward once he was free. We carried him out of the water and onto the shore, following Oliver towards the lit tree line to the left. Oliver remained ready to let loose his arrows in the event that whatever was making that shrill sound crossed our path. The sound followed us for some time before it finally faded into the background. Mabellio was doing a much better job at carrying Gavin than I was. I kept dropping my side and we'd all stumble a bit before we could continue on.

"Can we stop here?"

"No," Mabellio whispered. "We're still being watched. We have to get back to our home, and then Golar and the healers can help your friend."

I stopped short. "I don't want to go back there."

He gave me an odd look, but it was Oliver who responded. "Do you want Gavin to die?"

"No!"

"Then stop being so stubborn and belligerent and walk faster."

I wanted to lash out at him, retaliate at his brashness, but the sound of branches snapping held my opinions and my tongue. Instead, we all moved faster. When we reached the invisible entrance, Mabellio spoke two words in his language and we were instantly transported inside and finally sheltered from whatever it was that was following us. A small group of fae approached and took Gavin out of our hands. Each one examining him to see the nature of his injuries. The tallest male barked orders and the other male waved his hands in a crisscross fashion, literally raising Gavin from the ground until he was free-floating. The females proceeded to follow along beside him as they took him to a thatched hut off to the right. It was like a magical fairy version of the ER—two doctors and the nurses rushing to get their patient stable.

"Is he going to be all right?"

"They are our best healers. He should be fine," Mabellio said before gripping my shoulders. "I get that you are not from our world and do not understand what is surrounding you, but when Oliver and I tell you it's not safe, do not argue. Just move. You could have gotten us all killed."

"I—I didn't…"

"No, you didn't. If you run off again, I will not help to save you. I have a family of my own here, and while you are important, you are not more important than they are. Do you understand me?" Mabellio said in a firm but quiet voice.

I didn't reply, instead I just nodded my head. *What the hell was that out there and why was it so dangerous?* I wondered.

Mabellio walked away without another word, leaving Oliver and I alone. It was several long moments before Oliver finally turned to look at me. "You scared me, Novaleigh."

My eyes flashed to his, and I sunk to the ground. "Okay, but why?" I quipped as I put my hands in my hair.

"That man you met, the one with the pale, cracked face, was the Erlking. He is the warden of the in-between and he feeds off anger and pain. If we had not come along when we did, I don't know what he would have done to you." Oliver sighed. "Your energy was radiating so much, and he was looking at you as if you were his perfect meal."

I lifted my head to look at Oliver. "But he said he was after the one who hurt Gavin. I didn't hurt Gavin. I found him like that. Hell, I didn't even now that was him until I spoke to him. I just thought he was some injured man."

Oliver stared at me for a brief moment, as if he were trying to find the right words to explain the situation. He even opened and closed his mouth several times before he actually spoke. "Did you *ever* hurt Gavin, Novaleigh?"

My mouth gaped open. "Not physically," I stammered. "He and I…" I stood in one quick motion, feeling the need to run again. "It's a long story, and I don't want to talk about it, Oliver."

"I figured you'd say that," he said with a slight shake of his head. "We have to stay here until the Lunatishee find someone else to bother."

"The who?"

"Lunatishee. They guard the blackthorn trees and pay homage to the moon goddess with their efforts. Anyone who dares to take anything from their blessed tree is attacked. They are who was in the forest following us. They hate humans and relish the opportunity to poison them with the thorny spikes on their skin," Oliver explained as he sat down beside me. "But their poison can affect us too, just differently than your kind."

"I'm sorry," I whispered. "Will Gavin die?"

"I can't say for certain, but he was in bad shape."

I bit my bottom lip, hoping to contain the ache in my chest. "Wait. I didn't touch any trees. Why would they have attacked?"

"You didn't, but the Erlking did. He loves to cause mischief. He cut the branches and used them to bind Gavin. Then, all he had to do was wait. Gavin would be attacked and his pain would fuel the Erlking for a time, but then you came along."

"But how did he know I would come along, or anyone for that matter?" I questioned.

"Energy. Sacrife is a mecca for it. All things here emit some sort of frequency, some more than others. When you ran out of Golar's home and left the security of this place you offset the balance. The rift is what he felt, then you, along with the Lunatishee, became his pawns."

"Can I go home now? Please?"

He grinned slightly. "No. Not until you acknowledge your pain and move passed it."

"This is crap, Oliver. I don't want to face anything. I don't need to be fixed."

"Novaleigh, you have fallen out of focus. Lost sight of who you are and what you truly want to be. You've lived too long with the idea that your choice to follow your career was the correct one."

"How do you know this?" I whined.

He gave me a sideways glance. "I told you. You told us all when you were in your dream state. It was never our intention to spy, but you were talking in your sleep. It's normal for your kind to work through your pain in your dreams," Oliver offered.

I wrung my hands together. "I hate that I did that."

"But you did, so let me help you."

"Okay. Fine. Then please tell me why choosing myself for once in my life and wanting to pursue my dreams was a bad decision?"

"It wasn't. You lost your way when you made it the most important thing in your life. Tell me this, what did you lose when you made the choice to leave Scotland and go to New York?"

I swallowed hard. *What the hell?* Was fairy wine a friggin' truth serum too? It's like I spilled my guts. Hell, I never even kept a diary for fear that someone might stumble upon it one day and instantly know all my deepest and darkest secrets, and yet three glasses of fairy wine and I'd sang like a damn canary?

"A lot. My best friend for one, and then my mom was disappointed when I decided to move back to New York with my dad instead of following her to Glasgow. By that time they were officially divorced. Part of me blamed her for him leaving, but I realized after a while why my mom had had enough." I shifted on the ground and made myself a little more comfortable. *Guess it's truth telling time.* "My dad was temperamental and wanted to live a life without any attachments. At first, he wanted me to come with him to spite my mom, but when the reality of him having to manage a not-quite-adult set in, he found it tiresome. He was gone more than he was around. I eventually graduated from college and found a great job and moved out. He was elated. It was then that I knew beyond a shadow of a doubt that my mom had chosen to live her life in peace instead of according to my dad's whims."

"That's a lot in and of itself, but that was not all, now was it?" Oliver asked.

"No." I bit my lip again. "When I left Scotland, I left my grandparents and Gavin too." I looked over at Oliver, hoping to be able to stop at that first batch of truth, but instead of a pass, he just waited silently for me to continue. "You're not gonna let me off with anything brief are you?"

He shook his head. "Sorry."

"I was very close to my grandparents, and I spent almost every day with them. They were my dad's parents, but my mom was close to them too. In fact, she was closer to them than they were to their own son. He was distant and cold. My mom and I were warm and loving. It was the perfect combination. When my dad left, they were my mom's support system. She was American but moved to Scotland and gained her citizenship after a time. She's a professor at the University of Glasgow. She's an amazing artist and a wonderful teacher. Her students adore her." I smiled.

"Why did you choose your father over her then?"

I sat for a moment, pondering Oliver's question. Why had I chosen him over her? I didn't really have a reason. I'm very close to my mom. I talk to her all the time, and she's always been my biggest advocate, even when I pushed her away. I was angry, though, and had wanted to lash out. I chose to take it out on her. "What is it that they say? You always hurt the ones you're closest too or something like that." I choked on my words. "She was my safe place to fall, but I didn't want anyone to catch me then, I just wanted to run."

Two female fairies flitted towards us, waving their arms frantically and talking in a squeaky high-pitched tone that was practically inaudible. I assume it was harder to understand them since they were their true size as opposed to mine, but Oliver seemed to make out what they were saying and stood to follow them. When I didn't move right away, Oliver gave me a dirty look and waved me on.

"Sorry. Coming," I sassed.

We finally made it to a clearing and continued to follow the fairies as they flew to a large cottage. Mabellio and Golar were waiting near the door when we got there. My heart sank the moment I saw their faces.

"What's wrong? Where's Gavin?"

Mabellio grabbed my shoulders as I tried to barge through the door. "He's fine." He paused. "Now."

"Oh my God," I cried. "I want to see him."

Golar spoke in a calm, soothing tone. "You may, but understand he will need time to heal before he can journey anywhere. You both are welcome to stay, along with Oliver, of course, until he is able."

I nodded my head quickly. "Thank you." I started to walk through the doorway but turned back towards Golar and Mabellio. "Do you know how or why he is even here? I am

71

utterly confused. This is my dream. My nightmare. How is he a part of that?"

"I'm not certain I can answer that, Novaleigh, but I suspect that you can," Golar replied.

"Me? How would I know? I don't even understand how *I'm* here." I shook my head in confusion and pushed open the door. I walked down a small corridor and saw him lying there, on a wooden bed. There were fairies flying around checking him every few seconds. It was odd and confusing and while my mind was trying to comprehend what was happening, the logical part of my brain was trying to connect the dots to something realistic. The way Gavin was laying, slightly propped up, and the way they were caring for him, it seemed as though it was hospital of sorts. *I am seriously losing my mind. Yes, my best friend, sort of almost fiancé, is lying here in a fairy hospital in the middle of who knows where, being treated for wounds in a land I've created in my mind. Yep, totally lost it. Congratulations on your insanity, Novaleigh. You've hit the jackpot this time.*

A human looking fae walked in as I stood next Gavin. At first he didn't even acknowledge me but finally looked in my direction. "Is he going to be okay? He hasn't opened his eyes," I asked.

"The wounds on his wrists were deep and infected, but we gave him a special mixture of turmeric, goldenrod, and yarrow. Also, Golar used her healing magic to help speed up the healing in his entire body. I'm not sure when he will wake, but he was calling out your name earlier. It will be good for him that you're here."

I reached for Gavin's hand, careful not to touch the blend of leaves and flowers covering his gashes, and held it. I needed to feel him, know he was real. He stirred but immediately fell quiet again. The male fae started to walk out of the room, but I stopped him. "Thank you."

He gave a clipped nod and left Gavin and I alone.

I rubbed my thumb over the back of his hand. "How did we get here?"

Chapter Nine

Mom: I'm sending you a plane ticket.

I slowly reached for my phone and texted my mom back.

Novi: Mom we've talked about this and I'm too old to move home and mooch off you. I'll get it together. Promise.

Mom: Nonsense. It will only be temporary. I know you're just in a tough spot at the moment, and I want to help.

I stared at her words, knowing she was right but was unwilling to admit it to her or myself. I guess I took too long to respond to my mom's texts because the next ones came in rapid succession.

Mom: I think you need to go 'home' to renew yourself.

Mom: *The house is empty right now, and I can make one quick call and have Duncan get the place ready for a visit.*

Mom: *You can stay as long as you want. No strings attached.*

Mom: *And before you say no again, remember it was always the place that centered you.*

Tears started to well in my eyes. She was right—again.

'Home' was Scotland. Not where I was born but where my heart was. It was, and always will be, the place I loved most in the world. Words like peace and tranquility were what came to mind when I thought of the Isle of Skye.

Novi: *I want to, Mom, but I have bills to pay, and I really need to keep searching for a new job. Let me think about it.*

Novi: *And thank you, Mom for always believing in me! ILY*

Mom: *Love you too, Novaleigh.*

Wow, she must really be worried if she's using my full name in a text. Guess I should do more than just think about her offer, but it wasn't without its hassles. Leave my apartment, find someone to water my plants, and travel across the world just for some "R and R"? I mean, it seems a bit extreme when you think about it. I had just hit a rough patch. I can handle it. This too shall pass, and I'll find an even better job.

I rolled over and stared at the clock. 10:43 am. Usually, by this point in my day, I would've already answered all my emails, checked off half of my "to do's", and started on the latest manuscript in the slush pile. A slush pile so large that I had to move it from the wooden inbox on my desk to an actual box I set on the floor next to the window in my office. It was always there, looming over me, but it never felt like work. I loved it when another manuscript was dropped off, awaiting perusal and approval. In fact, I got a kick out of the different ways authors used to get someone to notice their work above all the others in the stack. I'd make it a game— finish a book, draft my notes into a Word.doc and attach them to the front with a sticky note before handing them over to their next destination. Some went to Mr. Kline for further review, while some went to Susan to fill in the proper names in the rejection form letter.

At that point I'd play "Eeny, meeny, miny, moe" to choose my next read. I had to read them all and deciding who was worthy of being read first seemed heartless to the author who had spent countless hours writing what they believed to be a perfect masterpiece. So instead, I let fate decide what book I would delve into. I gave each one my undivided attention, and since I was a speed reader, I could go through at least three books a week, if not more. But now, here I am, staring at the clock and wondering if I had anything edible in my fridge to have for a snack.

I picked up my phone again, paused, and then acted. Enough was enough.

Novi: Please tell me how much the ticket costs and you have a deal."

I hit the send button and sighed. Admitting defeat was not my strong suit.

Mom: Pay the courier when they deliver the package and we'll call it even. :P And if you are still there, I'll join you over the spring holiday. OXOXO

I grinned.

Novi: Well, hopefully I'll have my act together before then, Mom, but if not, I'd love to spend some time with you. I miss you terribly. I think the last time we were there together was at Nanna's funeral. Better memories would be great.

Mom: Yes they would. I'll see you soon and talk to you sooner. Got to run. Class is about to start.

Novi: <3

I looked around my apartment and wondered where to start first. The temperatures in Scotland this time of year were not too different from the temperatures here in New York, but I may need a few things I wouldn't need here. Time to make a shopping list.

"Novaleigh. Novaleigh," Oliver repeated as he shook me awake. "Let me sit with Gavin and you go get some rest." I shook my head, but he insisted. "Please. You're talking in your sleep again," he said with a sad smile.

I hadn't even realized I fell asleep. I looked up and saw Mabellio waiting by the door. "Let me escort you to your temporary dwelling."

I nodded sleepily and walked to meet him. "You know, I've taken a lot of your time today. Your family must be missing you."

Mabellio grinned. "My wife is an understanding woman, her and the children."

"Nonetheless, please thank her for me. I don't know how I could ever repay everyone's kindness here."

"That's not how we are, Novaleigh. We do things because it's the right thing to do, not because we're expecting something in return," Mabellio replied.

I smiled. "My nanna used to say that too."

He turned and led me towards a large oak tree at the edge of the clearing. It was a massive tree with a window jutting out of the middle of it. It even had a lit lamp post out front and a door that maybe came to my waist with a knocker handle in the center. I looked at him and he leaned down to open the door.

"It's bigger than it looks. The stairs will take you upstairs to the main dwelling. Oliver or I will come get you if there is any change in Gavin. Please just rest. No offense, but you look exhausted."

I could only imagine how I looked if it compared to how I was feeling. I'd tried to be strong for so long and it was catching up with me. The world felt heavy, and I'd been carrying it for some time now. Mabellio was right. I needed to sleep. On the upside, maybe I'd wake up and be home and Gavin would be safe and sound in Scotland.

"Thank you again, Mabellio."

"I'll see you in the morning."

My brows creased in confusion. "What time is it anyway?"

"It's the middle of the night."

"Wow, okay. I do need some sleep."

"The lights will go out once you're in bed. Offsemar will turn them out for you. He is our night fairy and the watchman over the village. You're safe here, Novaleigh. Find peace in that."

I pulled down on my sleeves, trying to cover my hands before I crossed them over my chest. "I'll try."

I closed the door and walked up the stairs where an open spacious living room awaited me. It wasn't just a living room, though, it had a huge canopy bed draped in layers of soft fabric. It looked like a small loft apartment and reminded me of my friend's place in Soho. The room was a mixture of eclectic and earthy, clean and simple, but homey. It was beautiful. Little white lights were draped in the rafters and lit the room with a soft glow. Mabellio may have been right. I was safe here, or a least I felt like it in this moment.

I slipped out of my shoes and ran my hands over the fur blanket at the edge of the bed. My eyes were weary just thinking about falling into its coziness. I pulled back the covers and slid into the most perfect bed I think I'd ever slept in. I sighed, closed my eyes, and let my mind wander. I needed to understand how I got here. I needed to retrace my steps that led me to this place—led Gavin and I to this place more accurately.

Chapter Ten

The journey home to Scotland had been long and arduous, but I had made it. I was home, well not technically, but certainly the place where my soul sang. I recalled the nightmares that brought me here; Mr. Kline and Ethan...Ethan would call daily begging me to forgive him with grand gestures of his love in the form of floral arrangements. As if flowers could erase the memory of your boyfriend banging his intern. All while Mr. Kline continued to pull strings behind closed doors that continued to leave me on the unemployed list. The hits just kept coming.

I found out right before I left that Mr. Kline had told everyone I intentionally deceived him regarding the state of the manuscripts I reviewed. According to him, I gave him the worst and passed on the best, selling them to other publishers

81

for cash. A bold face lie if I'd ever heard one. There was one manuscript, which I loved, but was wickedly reprimanded by Mr. Kline for even suggesting it go to print. I loved the story so much that after he declined it and the rejection letter was sent, I made a brief call to a competing agency to let them know the authors name and book title. All I did was simply say "it might be something they should read for themselves." It was not my fault Kline passed on it and it became a *NYT* Bestseller. He was the fool, not me.

However, I only did that once. Mr. Kline was implying I had made a habit of it and took cash for it to boot, and now publishing houses and agents were second guessing whether or not they should hire me. I was officially blackballed for being wise enough to see talent when I read it. I couldn't help but wonder if this was the final shoe—the last of my bad luck. Problem was, that even if it was the end, I was still in the same position. Jobless. So, I packed up and took my mom's offer and went home to Scotland to get my shit together.

"Miss, we're almost here," the driver said as we turned onto the road toward the main house.

I was immediately filled with emotion, some joyous, while others were nothing but sorrow. This home and this land would always hold both joy and sorrow for me. So many memories began here and ended here. I hope my mother was right that this place would center me so I could get back on my path.

The car slowed then stopped just as a mist of rain started to fall on the windshield. "Let me grab an umbrella for you."

"That won't be necessary. I don't mind getting wet," I replied as I rummaged for some cash. "Thank you so much for bringing me here." I paused. "I'm so sorry, I never asked you your name."

"Brody Andarsan. Pleased tae meet ye."

"Pleased to meet you as well, Mr. Andarsan."

"Brody," said as he helped me out of the backseat.

"Thank you."

"No one has been here in such a long time. Are you kin or have they taken to renting out the place?" he asked as he unloaded my bags from the trunk.

"Neil and Maureen were my grandparents." I smiled. "And I'm fairly certain if someone were to try and rent this house, they would come out of the grave to haunt us all."

We both laughed and made our way to the porch.

"Aye, then you must be Novaleigh. The whole town knows of ye."

"Oh, well that can't be good."

Brody grinned. "No, your mother and grandparents only spoke well of ye. It's nice to put a face with the stories."

"If you say so," I said as I handed Brody a handful of cash. "I hope the rest of your day is blessed and not too wet."

"Thank ye. Stay dry yourself."

I waited until Brody turned the car around and headed back down the road before I removed the brick hiding the key in the stone facing. As I turned the lock, the door opened outward without me doing a thing. What the…

"Gavin?"

"Novaleigh!"

"What are you doing here?"

"Well, I could ask the same. I thought I was preparing the place for your mom."

"Wait, what? Where is your father?"

"I've been helping him out lately," he said as he moved out of the way to let me in. "What brings you here? I thought you were in New York."

I grabbed one of my bags and stepped into the house just as Gavin moved to pick up the other two sitting on the step. "I was but had a few things happen that had me needing to make some changes. I'm just here for a bit."

"I'm sorry to hear that," Gavin said as he set the bags in the hallway.

I turned and looked at him. It had been years since I'd seen Gavin, and despite the scruffy beard and long hair he was sporting, he looked the same. *Deep set crystal-green eyes and dark brown hair with a hint of curl now that it was longer.*

"You're staring, Novaleigh."

I blushed and stepped toward him. "Sorry. I'm just intrigued by this new do of yours." I reached for his hair. "Weren't you always against the ragtag look?"

Gavin moved a bit closer, leaving only an arm's length distance between us. "Things change and so have I."

"Time has a way of doing that." I sighed.

"It's good to see you, Novi."

"Good to see you too, Gavin."

"I've got to be on my way. If you need anything, you know the number."

I bit my lip. "Yep. Got it."

Gavin turned to leave, and I was right behind him so I could close the door when he walked out, but he stopped short and turned back around. I bumped straight into him, our faces close, too close, at this point.

"I've missed you," Gavin whispered.

I stood there, stock still, and unsure of what to say. I mean, I had a lot to say but wasn't sure of the right words to use to explain how I truly felt.

"I didn't really think I'd see you again, but now that you're here maybe we can have a pint and...you know, catch up."

I swallowed hard. "I don't know, Gavin. I'm kind of screwed up right now, and I don't know that I'm in a good place mentally for anything. You'd do best to steer clear of me to be honest."

"You said that last time too, and yet here we are again at a crossroads." He kissed me on the cheek. "I think I'll let fate decide where this is going instead." He smiled and walked out the door.

Tears filled my eyes the moment he left. The history between us was long. We grew up knowing one another, remained close friends until the day we crossed that friendship line and tried for something more. In the beginning it was perfect, until it wasn't. I struggled with us being more. I'd lived in the states when all this started. Summer loves were always romantic but incredibly unrealistic when summers eventually ended and our lives would carry on but never in the same place. We loved each other for sure, but I was convinced we couldn't last. When my mom and I permanently moved to Scotland, Gavin and I were sophomores in high school. We were young and naïve, and no more than two characters in a romance novel living in a dream. The moment I took off the rose-colored glasses and started to see the relationship for what it was, I got cold feet.

Mom had moved to Glasgow and taken the professor position she was offered, and Dad was still back in New York doing his usual odd jobs here and there. It was then that I decided to make the move to New York. I thought if I had one more summer with Gavin I could ease out of "us", but that wasn't how it all happened. Gavin had made plans for us—permanent ones.

I would go with him to the University of Glasgow. I'd be close to my mom and we'd be together. I don't know that I can really say why I left like a chicken shit and ran back to New York without saying goodbye, other than I wanted to rebel against anything and anyone who wanted to control my choices. I was angry at my parents. Mad that my world had to be flipped on its axis because they couldn't get along. It was stupid and selfish, but that's what we are when we're in our late teens. We think we know everything but we don't. We're clueless. I had to learn the hard way. I wanted my lessons served with sharp, jagged edges. I started at NYU and pretended that Gavin and I were just nothing more than a young crush. I told myself that lie every day for the next seven years. Then I met Ethan, and well, we all know how well that worked out.

Gavin, according to my nanna, was heartbroken when I left and moved to Glasgow anyway to get his degree in business management. My grandparents were close with his family, so whenever I talked to them, they'd make sure to fill me in on Gavin's life, and I can only assume they filled him in on mine. Though, back then, I doubted he cared very much, since I'd hurt him so badly. However, the way he acted just now towards me has me wondering.

My nanna always said Gavin was the one who saw the real me and cherished it; that he was my querencia. At the time, I dismissed her notions, but as I dated other men and moved on through life's challenges, I realized that she may have been right. Gavin had always been there for me, was always a constant I could count on, and I foolishly dismissed him as a childish love. Truth be told, he meant way more than that to me, I was just never honest enough with myself to admit it. Odd how fate has brought me once again into his path and at yet another crossroad in my life.

A knock at the door startled me. "Novi, it's me. I forgot to open the chimney flue, and I don't want you to be smoked out of the house tonight," Gavin said through the closed door.

I wiped my eyes from the tears that were dampening my cheeks and unlocked the door. "Thank you. You know I would've stood there dumbfounded, trying to figure it out."

He laughed. "Maybe I should've left it then, and you would've had to call me to save you." I grinned and shook my head as he moved towards the drawing room. "But then again, I know how much you hate the idea of needing to be saved and spared us both the frustration."

I shook my head slowly, knowing that is exactly how I would have felt. "Then I guess my thank you will have to suffice then."

Gavin gave a clipped nod and then moved to open the flues in the rest of the house. When he opened the other two he turned to look at me. "Why have you been crying?"

"I—I haven't been."

"You stutter when you lie."

I sighed. "This house. You. The memories within these walls. Pick one, they're all catalysts."

"I get the other things, but why me?"

"Because, I'm sorry Gavin. Sorry I hurt you all those years ago. You didn't deserve it."

I think Gavin was taken aback by my words because now it was he who was stammering for something to say. "Guess that was just our destiny or fate or whatever they call it," he replied as he headed for the door. "Don't let the memories of any of this drown you, Novi. Our lives have unfolded as intended—life, death, love, loss, they are all part of it."

Tears spilled from my eyes. "Yeah, I guess so."

Gavin turned to look at me. "Whatever has brought you here can be healed, you just have to let yourself be vulnerable enough to allow it." He turned the handle and walked out the door without another word, leaving me shattered.

I could see in his eyes the desire to comfort me, but his pain held him in place. Maybe I'm the problem. Had I pushed Ethan away too and into the arms of his intern? Was my resistance to not wanting to be controlled the reason I was now jobless too? It's not unreasonable to believe I was the cause of all my problems. My pride and my ego were often in my way, but I could argue it's in most twenty-five-year olds way, right? Don't we all believe we have the world by the balls until something happens to show us *otherwise? I locked the door again, sure that Gavin wouldn't be returning tonight and took my bags to the upstairs guest room.*

Two and a half glasses of wine and a lingering fire had a way of warming the soul, well, not really, but at this point I could convince myself of anything. In reality, all I'd managed to do was dull the pain that wanted to consume me. Gavin's words had opened old wounds. Little fissures cracking and splitting, threatening to release all I've tried so hard to contain. I'm breaking even though I know I can't allow it. I must be strong. My emotions need to hold. This is just another moment in time. Another road to travel. These past few weeks would not define me anymore than my past would. I made choices, not always the right ones, but I made choices, and now here I am face to face with some of them.

A knock at the door woke me, and I stumbled out of bed and down the stairs to the door. When I opened it there were four fae women holding trays filled with food and drink.

"Good morrow, miss. We bring you nourishment and good tidings this day," the tallest one said with a cheerful grin.

"Yes, and information about your friend," the blonde one blurted.

"He is well," the ginger haired one interrupted. "Sir Oliver said to bring you over to the clinic once you were finished eating and ready for the day." She smiled wide.

I chuckled and stepped aside for them to enter. "This is very kind of you. It smells delicious."

"You must eat everything or else we cannot take you out," the last fae woman said in a shy but loud whisper.

"Okay, then I guess I better get started." I sat down at the mushroom shaped wooden table. "What do we have here?" I asked as I smelled the drink in the leaf cup.

"Fairy wine," they exclaimed.

"Oh no! Not touching that. Last night I didn't do so well on your fairy wine."

They frowned. "I guess we can make an exception," the tall one said as she snapped her fingers at the blonde. "Go get some blueberry juice. That will be perfect instead."

In an instant the blonde changed into her true size and flitted off to grab the juice.

"You didn't have to do that. I was fine with all this." I smiled.

"'Blueberry juice will cure all that ails, miss."

I sighed. "All right. Fair enough." I started to eat the biscuits and berries and closed my eyes when the flavors burst in my mouth. "Oh my gosh, this is heavenly."

The fae women collectively beamed.

The blonde returned shortly thereafter, carrying a glass bottle filled with a bright purple liquid. "Sorry I took so long. I had to squeeze you a fresh batch," she said as she handed it to me. "I hope you like it."

"I can assure you that if it's anything like the food you all have brought, I will love it," I replied as I took the bottle from her.

The four fairies tidied the room as I got my act together. They didn't have mirrors here, but I did my best to make myself feel presentable. I felt like a truck hit me, but there was no time to dwell on that. I wanted to get to the clinic and check on Gavin. I think it's time to try and explain to him why I treated him the way I did all those years ago. I thanked the fae women again as I headed down the stairs and out the door. I hoped Gavin was awake and ready to see me like he was when I first got home to Scotland. However, at this point, all I had was hope.

Chapter Eleven

When I walked down the corridor to where I'd last seen Gavin, my hands began to shake. *Why was I so nervous?* It was Gavin for crying out loud. The person who knew me best in this world. The closer I got, the slower I walked. *You can do this.* The clinic was buzzing today with fae—men and women, human sized and fairy sized alike. They were not busy with patients but rather were working in groups to make what look like medicine. Flowers and roots were being cut and crushed into powders and gels, while others were being held over small flames. *Wow. I guess this really is a hospital of sorts.*

I continued to walk until I found where Gavin and Oliver were. He must've been well enough to move him because they were both sitting in a well-lit room with couches and chairs.

"Hi," I said to them both .

"Good morning, Novi," Oliver replied.

Gavin looked up at me and then turned away. My palms starting sweating. This was the reception I expected from him in Scotland, but no, instead, I got to experience his cold shoulder now, here in this bizarre place. *You deserve anything and everything he gives you.*

"It's good to see you up and around, Gavin," I struggled. "And how are you this morning, Oliver?"

"I'm well," Oliver replied as he took a sip from the cup in front of him. "You still look tired."

"I slept some," I said as I fidgeted with my shirt and looked for a place to sit, or if I was truthful, hide.

Oliver took another sip of his drink and then stood. "I think I'll go get some rest myself. I'm certain you two have a lot to talk about," he said before he took his leave.

The air was thick and heavy between Gavin and me. He continued to stare out the window, and I felt nauseous. We were quite the pair. My voice cracked. "So how…how are you feeling?"

He didn't turn to look at me. Instead he just mumbled. "I'm fine."

"I was surprised to see you here," I stammered. "How are you here?"

He scoffed. "Sorry. Didn't mean to intrude upon you." He finally looked my way, but now I was wishing he'd continued to stare off into the distance. He was angry, and I didn't really blame him, but…well, I wanted this to be a civil conversation.

"That's not what I meant. I—I just didn't expect to see you here and bound in a swamp."

"It wasn't a swamp and how do you know I didn't want to be there?"

I flinched. "What? What is that supposed to mean?"

"It means, Novaleigh that the hell I was in," he paused, "currently in, is better than the hell I was in when you left me."

Dagger. Heart. Soul.

I looked away. "I know. I'm sorry," I mumbled.

"Sorry. You're sorry? For what exactly?" he snapped. "Never having the guts to tell me the truth? Leaving and never calling to explain that you're selfish and self-serving? Or simply sorry."

Tears started to stream down my face. What could I say back? He was right on all counts. I was all of those things and more. I wiped my eyes before the drops slid down my chin. They were coming faster now, though, the more I let Gavin's words sink in.

"I'm sorry, Gavin. I truly am."

"I'm sure you are, Novaleigh, but it changes nothing."

"You're right," I struggled. "I'll leave you be."

He scoffed and moved to stand but lost his footing. I was close enough to catch him which was helpful but not wanted. As soon as he could, he pushed out of my arms and used the back of a chair to steady himself. "I don't want or need your help anymore. We may be here in this place together, but that is just geography. You need to go and find your way away from me, away from here."

I nodded. "Understood."

Gavin limped over to the window and turned his back to me. This was exactly what I expected, and I didn't bother to argue. I moved to leave but paused before I made it to the opening to the corridor. "I didn't know that you were the man bound. I just wanted to help. When I found out it was you...I couldn't let you suffer. I'm just glad you're okay."

Silence.

I left without another word.

As I stepped out of the clinic and back out into the open space of Cadent, I pondered what to do next. I was infamous for running, burying my pain and pretending like everything was okay, when actually, I was unsteady and falling apart. This time, I needed to make smarter choices. I could run now, or I could think where I should go next to get out of this insanity and back to some semblance of a real life. I walked towards a group of fae males farming and asked if they knew where I could find Oliver. At first they looked at me sideways, but when I explained I was looking for an overly dressed otter with glasses, they pointed me to a cottage at the end of the clearing. I walked for a while, picked a bunch of wildflowers, and finally made it to the place Oliver was staying. I knocked on the door and waited.

Oliver opened the door and looked up. "Are you okay?" he asked.

I nodded. "I am, but I want to leave. I think it's time to move on."

"What about Gavin?"

"He doesn't want me around, and it's probably for the best," I said with a curt smile. "Can we leave soon? Or can you point the way so I can go?"

"You know I can't do that, Novi. I have to go with you."

"I figured you'd say that. Can we leave soon then?"

"Depends on where you want to go next?"

"I wanted to go to the place I saw yesterday. The place where the trees were tall and frostbitten."

Oliver shook his head frantically. "No. We cannot go there, Novaleigh."

"Why not?"

"We cannot go to The White."

"The White? What does that mean?"

"It's official name is Hiems, but for all of us, we call it *The White*, it's not a good place and certainly not for you."

My shoulders dropped. "Not for me?"

"Yes, Novi. Not for you," he emphasized as he pulled me down towards the porch of his temporary cottage. "And this is not a challenge. I've figured out by now that when someone tells you not to do something, it's the first thing you want to do. That is not what this is. Ninety percent of the inhabitants of Sacrife, not just those who live here in Cadent, avoid that area at all costs. It is not safe."

I thought about what he was saying and nodded my head slowly in agreement. "So then I guess you need to tell me where we are going next then."

"Well, first I must ask why you are ready to leave Gavin? He has not yet healed completely."

"I already told you. He doesn't want or need me. I need to move on so I can get back to my home, where I come from."

"Then I think *Awakening* is where you need to go next. We call it that because it is what happens in Hortus, and while that name doesn't exactly elicit positive thoughts, that is exactly what Hortus is. There is new life there. Beauty at every turn. I think you will like it there, Novi."

I nodded again but was silently disappointed. Was I ready for an awakening? Did I really want new life? I mean, yes, of course that is a step in the right direction, but I couldn't help shake the feeling I had more to do before I was truly ready to start again.

"When can we leave?" I relented.

"It's a two-day journey, and it's mid-morning now. Let's eat lunch and we can set out after that. This will give us a chance to find shelter before darkness falls."

"All right, we leave after lunch."

"I will speak with Golar and Mabellio and ask them to help gather what we may need for our journey. You should probably go back to your dwelling and rest. This journey is a bit more treacherous than the one that brought us here."

I leaned over and hugged him then stood to leave. I really didn't have much to say. I just wanted to get back to Scotland and out of this fantasy. As I walked back towards my assigned dwelling, I looked in the direction of the clinic. My heart ached, and I clenched my fists to stave off the pain of his rejection. *Again, you only have yourself to blame, Novaleigh.*

Lunch wasn't just cheese and crackers. No, it was a massive feast like the morning I arrived. Everyone in Cadent was in attendance Golar said. Apparently, they all wanted to wish me well on my journey to Hortus. I was overwhelmed by their admiration and gifts. At this point, I think I'll need two extra-large Samsonite suitcases to carry everything they were giving me.

Oliver bumped my arm. "Don't worry, we can pack all that to make it portable."

"Good thing. I was a bit worried, and I didn't want to offend anyone," I whispered.

"It's almost time for us to be heading out. Did you need to do or say anything to anyone before we leave?"

I narrowed my eyes at him. "Subtle, and no. Other than Golar and Mabellio, I'm good."

"Very well then," he said as he stood. "Give me five minutes, and I too will be ready. I left a few things in my room."

"How about I meet you at the tree over there with all the hanging lanterns then?" I pointed.

He adjusted his glasses and flicked a nod. "Five minutes."

I made my way over to Mabellio and his family. The kids were playing while a woman with long golden hair held an infant in her arms. "I wanted to say goodbye and thank you again for helping me."

"It was no trouble. Is your friend well?" Mabellio asked.

"He's well as far as I know." I forced a smile.

Thankfully, Mabellio didn't push and ask more questions, instead he turned to the woman standing beside him. "Novaleigh, this is my wife, Ilsepas."

I held out my hand and she looked at me funny, but she quickly smiled a smile that lit up her whole face. "It's wonderful to finally put a face with the name," she said as she leaned in to hug me. "I'm sorry we haven't met before now, but I've been tied up with the baby and unable to attend the events. I hope you have found what you were looking for during your visit here." Ilsepas pulled away when the baby stirred in her arms.

"She's beautiful. How old is she?"

"Twelve days today." She beamed.

"Holy Hannah. You look great, and she looks like a perfect blend of the two of you." I smiled. "It was lovely to meet you, Ilsepas. Your husband was too kind, and I won't soon forget it. Please be well—all of you."

After another round of hugs, I made my way over to Golar. She was sitting, not in a throne as you would expect from a queen, but in a high back chair covered in a burnt orange mushroom cloth and that had sunflowers and marigolds scattered about. The chair alone was a work of art, but as I looked at the queen sitting in it, I was reminded of the Celtic goddess my nanna used to read me stories about. Golar was every bit as beautiful. As I got closer, I realized she was talking to another fae. I waited until she was finished and approached. "Please pardon the interruption, but I wanted to say goodbye and thank you. Oliver and I will be leaving shortly, and I couldn't leave without expressing my appreciation."

She reached for my hands. "It was our pleasure, Novaleigh. I wish you well on the next leg of your journey. Will Gavin be joining you and Oliver?"

"No. He has chosen to go his own way. Thank you, though, for healing him. I—I would be heartbroken if something happened to him," I stammered.

"He may be closed off to you at this moment, Novaleigh, but have faith. What is meant to be will be."

I tried not to show any physical signs of mental anguish out of respect, but inside I was screaming at her words. *Yeah right. He would walk past me and let me die if he ever saw me again. That ship has sailed. In fact, it's been gone for years.*

She squeezed my hands and smiled. "It may seem as though all hope is lost, but sometimes people surprise you."

"Wait, I hadn't said that out loud."

Golar smiled again. "I know."

I sighed.

I looked up and saw Oliver waving me on. "I have to go, Golar. I wish I knew a way to repay you for your kindness."

"That's not necessary. All I ask is that you keep your heart open to new possibilities and to stop letting the past control your future decisions. Each day is a new chance to make better choices. Do that for me, and I will always be filled with peace."

I nodded solemnly and then hugged her before rushing off to meet up with Oliver.

"Are you ready to go?" Oliver asked.

"Yes."

I took one last look at the clinic and felt that ever present tug in my heart. At least here he was safe. I wished him well and turned to leave. There in the window, the sun obscuring parts of him, was Gavin, looking at us as we headed for the portal. I waved a hand, knowing it wouldn't be reciprocated. It was okay though. I was saying goodbye. Now if only I could get my heart to listen to the sanity behind the gesture.

Oliver and I stepped out of the peace of Cadent and back onto the main road in Sacrife. I had no idea what two day's journey was going to feel like, but we were moving on. In a way, it felt good—sad but good.

Chapter Twelve

The sky in Sacrife was as it was the first day I arrived. The only difference today was that it seemed darker and more ominous. The trees were barren and with dusk approaching they began to loom over us like soldiers guarding the path. Oliver and I stayed close to one another, but the air had shifted, leaving us both a tad uneasy.

"The road to Hortus will skirt the outer banks of Hiems so be aware of your surroundings," he said flatly. "Also, there will be things trying to lure you towards the realm. Ignore them."

"You mean like Sirens?"

He gave me a quizzical look.

"Sirens are mythical creatures who lured sailors to their doom with their seductive singing." I smiled.

"I guess it could be something like that, but they won't sing. They will, however, try to trick you with things you are attracted to or have some connection to," Oliver replied.

I shrugged, dismissing his comments. I got it. DO NOT GO TO THE WHITE OR YOU WILL BE LOST. Oliver hadn't ever screamed it at me, but he'd certainly reiterated it enough that it felt like he had.

Darkness had set in, and Oliver had pulled yet another trick out of the satchel he carried and produced lanterns to light our way. We continued on our path for a while without incident, but I guess I willed it into existence, because suddenly, there was a roadblock before us. There on the side of the road was a broken-down wagon. It honestly looked like a Romanian gypsy wagon, sans the horse. It was brightly colored and decorated with a dozen or so round lanterns. I slowed but Oliver waved me on without a word. We almost made it past the back when the door opened and a wooden staircase dropped down out of the back of the wagon. In an instant, five harlequin-like clowns emerged and began to perform all kinds of acrobatic tricks, encircling us—correction...corralling us.

They were graceful but a little creepy too. They were wearing black and white costumes that were form fitting and appeared to move like some psychedelic drug trip when they flipped around. That of course was odd, but not nearly as odd as the chant they were singing as they continued to perform their tricks.

See us dance.
Watch us flip.
Care to take a chance?
We'll only need a sip.
Come to see our mistress?
Or come to see our master?
She can be quite viscous.
But he is a disaster.
We love them both, and we'll let you choose.
Either way, we wouldn't want to be in your shoes.

Chills ran up my spine as they continued to repeat it over and over again. What the hell was that screwed up rhyme supposed to mean? I looked down at Oliver who never took his eyes off the clown-like creatures as he rubbed the crystal he had hanging around his neck. He blew on the clear jagged shard until it began to glow vibrant shades of pink and purple. He reached for my hand, and I took it immediately. Something was about to happen, and I doubted it was going to be good. *Here we go again.*

Out of the wagon emerged a cloaked figure who was followed by a haunting woman. She was literally stark white— her hair, her skin, her eyelashes, her dress, and crown on her head. Everything was washed in white, except for her eyes. They were an icy-blue that made her appear ethereal but not in a good way. My heart was racing and with each breath I took, the wider she grinned. *Oh shit.* I tried not to look at her, but I couldn't take my eyes off her. What the hell was she? Who was she?

"Crossing a little too close, are you not, otter?" the woman said in a honeyed tone. "I think you owe us a passage payment."

"No. We have favor with the twin queens and that buys us a pass."

She hissed. "It buys you nothing."

"Lithia, do you dare anger Uphren? You know her temper when she is displeased," Oliver challenged.

Oliver suddenly dropped to his knees and made a gasping noise. I knelt down and screamed up at her and the cloaked figure. "ENOUGH!"

The woman, Lithia, spat her response. "You are nothing special. Pink hair or not."

"Yeah, no shit! I never said I was. Release him, now!"

The cloaked figure moved closer to me but was blocked from getting too close. Was I immune to their power but Oliver wasn't? No. I realized when the man looked at his hand as it flickered with ombre hues of fire. I gasped. *His hand...stark white, crackled like dried mud. Oh my god, the warden.* He pulled back the hood of the cloak and reveal himself. "We meet again."

Lithia released Oliver from whatever magical force she was choking him with and cast a glance at the warden. "You know this thing?"

"Hey!" I shouted before I could stop myself.

"You dare to speak to me in such a tone? I will have your head."

I rolled my eyes. *Hmm, wonder where I'd heard that phrase before?* "Where are your card soldiers and shouldn't you be shorter and a bit more red?"

Oliver's eyes went wide. "Novaleigh, stop. Do not aggravate her any more than she already is," he whispered into my ear as he tried to stand. "We are safe here on the main trail, but if the magic surrounding us ceases to hold, those creatures will have fun playing with us. Understand?"

I, too, stood and tried to compose myself. Sure, I was being a badass on the outside, but on the inside I was quaking in my boots. All I could think of was the phrase my dad's father used to say to him when I was a kid, *"Don't let your alligator mouth overload your hummingbird ass,"* and I think I'd done just that.

"We want to pass. We have no business or quarrel with you, Lithia. We'll just be on our way," Oliver said as he dusted off his trousers and adjusted his glasses.

He was sure and deliberate with his tone, but I suspected that he felt the same way I did—we were on thin ice and at any moment it could crack and then everything would change.

Lithia's demeanor changed and she made her way back over to the wagon. "Come forth," she bellowed to someone inside.

Chains rattled as someone appeared in the opening. A slender female with hair as pitch black as midnight, slowly made her way down the wooden ladder. She had tawny skin that was wrinkled and thinning. She looked like one of those apple face dolls, all weathered and worn.

"How may I serve you?" she asked when she finally stood beside Lithia.

"Her," Lithia pointed at me. "I want to know more about her?"

The old woman nodded. "From where I stand, she is lost, traveling in our lands to find her way home but cannot accept the truths before her. She believes we are all a dream and that we are just figments of her fractured mind. She is stuck between two worlds."

My eyes went wide. What the hell was that? How did she know that? I never said a word.

The woman's voice changed and she began to mimic my own. "I'm currently living in the space between lost and happy. It sounds odd I know, but it's truthful. I don't want to be in this limbo, but I am. The question is, how do I get back to happy?"

Oliver grabbed my hand and squeezed it will all his might. "Do not fall for it. It's a trick. The seer can only read echoes of your thoughts. Think of something happy or memorable, anything, and it will distract her."

Lithia's snarl became a grin. "This I can use."

"You will use nothing. I'm not falling for your shit," I snapped.

Lithia's laugh became a cackle as she gripped the chains binding the old woman and yanked them to her. "Find out more or I will use your daughter instead of you as my puppet."

The woman shook with fear. "But that is all I can see. The magic imbued around the girl makes it impossible to view anything more. Even if I held her hand, I would be blocked from her entire thoughts."

Lithia snarled and pushed the woman to the ground. "Useless."

The warden, who had been standing to the side of Lithia, kicked the old woman and called for two of the freaky acrobats to remove her from their sight. The poor lady moaned in pain and cried out loud when one of them bit her on the wrist. *Guess I now know what the clowns meant when they said they'd only needed a sip. Eeww.*

An electrical surge filled the air and Oliver's faced dropped.

"What is that?" I whispered.

"Your demise," the warden answered.

Lightening crackled in the sky above, just as the ground beneath our feet began to shake. Oliver and I were still holding hands, and I wasted no time. I tugged Oliver and took off running. I had no idea where I was headed, but at the moment, all I wanted was for Oliver and me to be as far away from Lithia and the warden as possible.

We ran, but it wasn't fast enough. Out of the sky a funnel cloud formed and appeared to follow us. If we zigged, so did it. It was as if it were honed in on us. The noise from the growing tornado was eerie. I'd always heard they sounded like freight trains, but now that I was experiencing one first hand, it was bone chilling. Like the train was the size of Texas, and it was barreling down on Oliver and I with a vengeance.

"WE NEED TO SPLIT UP!" I screamed at Oliver. "GO THAT WAY!"

He screamed back. "NO! WE CANNOT LOSE ONE ANOTHER."

The funnel cloud made the choice for us. One second we were a few feet from each other, and the next, I lost him in the whirlwind. The air went from cool to freezing in an instant. My teeth were chattering, and I was floating in the center of the cone. For a moment it was quiet, but as I was tossed around, the sound became deafening. Debris was flying around me, cutting my skin and my clothes. I tried to focus my thoughts, but I'd lost the ability to think logically. I was falling…again.

When I was tossed from the tornado, I landed in a snow drift that thankfully softened my fall. It took me a few moments to gather my wits, but when I was able, I realized I had to be in the one place Oliver told me not to go—Hiems. *Well, crap.*

Chapter Thirteen

It was so cold, my lungs were struggling to catch a breath. I rubbed my arms, hoping to warm myself, but there was no way with the clothes I was wearing I would be able to get warm. I needed to find shelter and soon. Darkness was settling in, and in just a short while I would be blind to my surroundings. The trees almost seemed to disappear against the skyline. There was nothing around for as far as the eye could see.

A light began to glow underneath the shirt I was wearing and extended outwards. The ombre shades of pink were glowing against the glittery snow, illuminating all the white. *Pink*. The twin queens must've been watching over me and sending me a sign that I wasn't lost. But wasn't I? *How are you going to get out of this, Novaleigh?*

"Fear"

"Not"

"Novaleigh."

"We"

"Are"

"Sending"

"Someone"

"To"

"Help"

"You."

I looked around and saw no one but knew by the broken sing-songy voices that it was them. How were they talking to me?

"We"

"are"

"with"

"you"

"always,"

"child."

A pitter-patter sound was coming up behind me, and I turned sharply to see what or who it was. There, coming at a steady pace, were several rabbits, but not just rabbits, rabbits with small elven fairies upon their backs. They were riding them as if they were horses.

"Hello, miss. We are here to show you the way. Come with us," one of them said excitedly.

I moved to stand, but fell immediately. Something must've happened to my ankle in all the ruckus, because the moment I put weight on it, it gave way.

I screamed out in pain and the fairies dismounted to run to my aide. "Where does it hurt?"

"Here," I cried.

The fairies ran down to my ankle and began working, doing what, I don't know, but within moments I went from mind numbing pain to something far more bearable.

"Better?"

I nodded.

"We need to get you to the hideaway before the sun completely sets, otherwise we are all in extreme danger. Can you try and follow us now? It is not far."

I nodded again. As I started to move, Oliver came running out of the tree line. *Oh, thank God.* He ran so fast that he was next to us in an instant. He was holding something in his hand and when he was standing close enough to touch me, he barked orders at the fairies who worked quickly to do as he asked. They mounted their rabbits, lined up and began to encircle us.

They had in effect, created a barrier between us and the rest of "The White" as Oliver called it.

"Now," he yelled at the same time he tossed the contents of his hand into the air.

The fairies each shot an arrow into the cloud of leaves and powder Oliver had just hurled upwards. Sparks flew and ember flames began to surround us.

"This only works once and will wear off eventually, but by then, we will be well on our way to Hortus. For now though, Lithia and the warden are close, and I need you to follow my friends to their hidden home, and I will find you later, okay?"

"What about you, Oliver?"

"I can remain hidden. You are harder to hide. Now please stop questioning me and go," he snapped.

"Fine," I breathed.

I lost track of all the events that happened next, but from what I can remember, one minute I was sitting in the snow and the next minute, a tree was growing up out of the ground, rising until it almost reached the sky. Near the top were houses built right into the trunk of the massive tree. These "tree houses" were different from the ones in Cadent. Their homes there were built into the bases of the trees, yet these were high up. I wondered why. I also wondered how I was going to fit considering I was a human and not six inches tall.

"Um, excuse me," I asked a mahogany skinned woman carrying a basket full of bright red apples. "I'm looking for the fairies that were riding the rabbits.

She shrugged and went on about her way.

"Please wait! I'm going to crush this place, and I don't want to hurt you all."

"Miss," a voice behind me spoke. "Why are you troubled?"

"I–I'm scared that I am too big to be here in your home."

"Why?"

My eyes went wide. "Look at me."

The elven fairy gave me a blank stare. "You look fine. Are you feeling ill?"

I was flabbergasted. "I'm huge, that's why!"

He still just stood there, staring at me blankly. "I'm afraid not, miss. You are the same as all of us."

"I'm not...wait, what?"

I looked down, and I was indeed not my normal size. I was the same height as the fairy before me. I shook my head in shock.

"Um...did I shrink?"

He smiled wide. "Yes, when we lit the spark. Oliver used his magic to change you."

I thought back to what Oliver had said in that moment. *"This only works once and will wear off eventually, but by then we will be well on our way to Hortus. For now though, Lithia and the warden are close, and I need you to follow my friends to their hidden home..."*

"So I'm not going to stay this size then?"

He laughed. "No, miss, you are not."

I blew out a puff of air, grateful for that. "I'm Novaleigh, by the way. And you are?"

"Neesweth," he beamed. "If you follow me I can take you to a more comfortable place. The main thoroughfare will be cluttered soon with everyone readying for the night shift."

"Oh. Okay," I replied as I followed Neesweth.

This place was so high up in the massive trees, it was like a rural fairy village suspended in the clouds. There were barns, stables, and livestock, along with all kinds of animals and gardens, as well as pathways and fences. And it was all small, well, would be small if I was regular size.

"Oh, miss. Please let me have the crystal you were using to illuminate The White. I shall need to charge it with the light of the moon, so if you ever need it again, it will be ready."

I put my hand around the cord holding the necklace and pulled it over my head. "Thank you. I didn't know it could do that."

"Ah yes, your queens' magic is vast and powerful."

"Oh, they are not my queens."

He chuckled again. "Of course they are. Why else would they risk so much to save you?"

I reached for his shoulder, halting him. "Risk? What did they risk?"

He stopped and stared at me curiously before speaking again. "The White is not for our kind to live in. We may hunt and forage during the day but when darkness begins to fall, we must be safely returned to our homes. Those are the rules."

I gulped. "May I ask you why?"

His eyes widened. "Oh, we dare not name it."

"Name what? And why?"

"For fear that naming it will call it to us."

"Aren't you hidden up here?"

"Yes, but their hearing is perfect and," Neesweth paused. "No, I cannot."

"Well, how can I know that I won't encounter whatever this is if you don't tell me what it is?"

121

Neesweth stepped close, very close and whispered hurriedly. "Lunatishee."

"The Lunatishee? I know them. They are what Oliver and Mabellio warned me about in Cadent. They're connected to Lithia, right?" Panic set in. I'd never actually seen one, but I'd never forget the sound of their shrill cries.

"Shhhh, never say their names. Oh dear, oh dear," he cried as he paced back and forth rapidly.

"I'm sorry. I'm so sorry. I will never speak their names again."

"The creature I named, they are many and they *are* bound to the will of the other name you will never speak of again. They are all beasts who roam the woods in search of food. They despise your kind the most, and you must avoid them at all costs, miss."

"Okay, I promise."

Neesweth shivered. "They're a dark green, almost black, and they're covered in thorny spikes that are poisonous to anyone who comes in contact with them," he said as he looked me straight in the eye, "but you will not encounter them because we are hidden from their view. Now enough of all this chatter. We dine when the moon is highest in the sky. Meet us in the dining hall, and I beg of you, do not mention this conversation to anyone. It could be our demise." He gave a clipped nod and began walking again.

"I understand."

He stopped abruptly in front of a glass door. "Here you go. This will be yours while you are with us."

I peeked through that glass and made a mental note not to stand near it once inside. "It is lovely.

"See you at dinner, Miss Novaleigh," he said with a slight bow.

I closed the door behind me and walked into the spacious room. It was not as I expected. This home was not made of wood, but grey stone. Dark mortar and olive colored moss filled in the spaces between the brick, giving it an eerie feel. This home was colder than the one I stayed in Cadent, but then again, we were high in the sky above The White. Maybe they needed the stone to provide them warmth. A fire was lit in the fireplace, not roaring, but it was enough to take the chill out of the air. As I took stock of the rest of the room, I was struck by the sharp contrast of the cold stone to the white wisteria hung in strands above the bed in the center of the circular space. It was beautiful and elegant and looked as if it belonged in a fairytale. *You're dreaming. You have been since you got here. Do not forget that or you truly will be lost*, I reminded myself.

I laid down on the bed and sunk into the cloudy center. It wasn't long before I drifted off to sleep and was heading towards yet another dreamland.

Chapter Fourteen

I woke to the floor rumbling beneath me and the glass door rattling in its frame. I tried to steady myself, but the bed started sliding from one side of the room to the other. What was happening? I didn't have time to think about that, because on one of the passes of the bed, it managed to bump into the wall with the lit fireplace. In an instant, flames shot up and the bed covering became engulfed. I jumped off the bed and tried to put the fire out, but it had gotten too big and there was no stopping it. All I could do was run out the front door and onto the path, but here in the open, it was far worse.

Everywhere I looked there were fairies screaming and running around, grabbing their children and/or animals. No one knew what to do. It was total chaos. Another quake and the tree dipped to the left, cracking and splitting in two.

Everyone was trying to grab something to hold onto, but it was no use. The tree was coming down. My heart was breaking as I watched the elven fairies lose their footing and fall into the darkness. Their hidden village was being destroyed, and they were being destroyed with it. I managed to find a branch to hang on to as we continued to descend. The lower we got, the easier it was to see who was terrorizing these poor fairies.

As balls of flames from the tree whizzed by, I caught glimpses of what could only be described as dark shadowy giants. Giants with large spikes running along their backs and trailing down to their long tails. *Oh shit, the Lunatishee.* I stared in disbelief. Everything seemed to be happening in slow motion as they slashed at the tree bark with their enormous claws. They were huge hulking creatures.

I held on and closed my eyes, willing myself to wake up from this terrifying dream. Neesweth and all of his family were perishing before my eyes. I never wanted to wake up more than I did in this very moment.

The Lunatishee had done all the damage they could do to the tree and began targeting the elven fairies who were just trying to save themselves. I braced myself when I saw white. I knew then that the tree was about to finally hit the ground. Many voices continued to scream while others became silent.

The large pile of fresh snow blanketed my fall and I sunk into its cold softness. I tried not to move. One of the Lunatishee was standing no more than three feet away, and I quickly realized they weren't giants at all, really. Had I been my usual size, I would be taller than them, but since I'm still only six inches at the moment, they definitely had the advantage.

I stifled a scream and lay motionless, hoping he wouldn't see me. Up close, I could see the details of the creature and it was just as Neesweth had described—dark green, almost black, and covered in thorny spikes. The Lunatishee's eyes glowed in the dark and appeared to be able to see everything that moved. I lay motionless, despite the fact that the frozen ground was chilling me to the bone. I remembered what Neesweth said about them being able to smell humans and couldn't for the life of me understand why it wasn't attacking me. Could the snow I was buried under be masking my scent? I had no idea, but I hoped whatever was protecting me from their wrath would continue to work.

There was a rustling in the trees beyond where I could see; the creature took notice and reached over its shoulder to pull one of its spikes from his back. It immediately grew another as it launched the one in its hand towards the sound. A loud moan and then a thud confirmed he'd hit his target. Another sound and the Lunatishee took off in its direction leaving me alone. I waited a few moments before I moved. When I heard nothing but silence, I peeked over the snow hoping they'd all gone.

Horror hit my soul. In the darkness, fires burned, illuminating the tragic scene. I could see bodies of the elven fairies, young and old. The Lunatishee had shown no mercy to the fae. There were animals and children unmoving all around. Tears filled my eyes as I looked in the direction I last heard a noise and saw what the Lunatishee had hit with its thorny spike—Neesweth and his rabbit. I ran over to them, trudging as best as I could through the densely packed snow. Neesweth was still breathing but only barely, while his rabbit lay lifeless next to him.

"I'm so sorry, Neesweth. So sorry."

"Are there any alive?" he choked.

"No," I whispered as a tear slid down my cheek. "What can I do for you?"

"Nothing I'm afraid. The poison has taken hold. I will not survive." I cried softly as I stared into his eyes. "Your crystal is in my rabbit's pouch. You," he coughed. "You need to take it and go. Run as far as you can and hide. The crystal will," he coughed again, "show you the path."

Trees snapped in the distance and we both froze.

Neesweth pulled me closer. "You must go now, miss. Don't let them get you," he said in barely a whisper.

I nodded and leaned over to find the crystal. I was so frightened and numb to all of what just happened. Had this been my fault? Would these people all be alive if it wasn't for me? Yet another thing I can add to my long list of guilt and angst.

"How did they find your hideaway?"

His sad eyes met mine once again. "You may be our size, miss, but you still smell like a human. They hate humans."

I closed my eyes and cried some more. It was my fault. *You did this Novaleigh. You killed an entire village of fairies.*

The slight rise and fall in Neesweth chest had stopped. He too was gone. I lay by his side for a few more moments, but when the sounds of branches cracking grew louder, I ran as fast as I could to the nearest brush and hid. Out of the barren forest came three Lunatishee. One was carrying a pouch at his hip, the second used a long stick to sift through the bodies, and the third picked up the villagers or the animals and shoved them in the first one's pouch. I had no idea what they were going to do with them and then the third one picked up Neesweth's rabbit and took a bite out of his side with its black fangs.

My stomach lurched. *Oh no. You cannot throw up. Keep it together. Think. Stay alive.*

I waited until the creatures had cleared the field of their "prizes" before I made my way in the opposite direction of where they were headed. I had no idea where to go or what to do. I was freezing. *Another right fucked situation.*

I looked at the path before me and wished I was a human size again. Making my way in a frozen tundra when you're six inches tall is not exactly possible when I'd already sunken below my head a few moments ago. My skin tingled and the hairs on the back of my neck stood on end. Suddenly, I was now taller than the bush and continuing to grow. I'd gone back to my full size, clothes, shoes, and all. *Be careful what you wish for around here.*

A loud shriek rang out in the distance. I guess with my increased size, came an increased scent too. *So much for the 'magic is hiding me' theory.* I took off in a dead run in the direction of a pinky-orange glow, hoping that it was a sign from the queens. *Help me, please.* I cried out in my mind. *PLEASE!*

Chapter Fifteen

I ran until I was out of breath. I knew I needed to keep going, but my side was cramping and my body was half frozen. The light I'd been running towards seemed like a mirage. No matter how far I ran, I was not any closer. I reached for the crystal around my neck and played with it for a few minutes. I had no idea how it worked and apparently talking to it, kissing it and/or praying to it had no real affect. It still remained dark. Had I fallen out of favor with the twin queens when the Lunatishee killed the elven village? I wouldn't blame them if that was the case. Since I'd been here in Sacrife, all I'd done was cause trouble. I guess my bad luck from home followed me to this place too. *Lucky them.*

The moon finally became visible as it shifted in the sky, and I saw the snow all around me. It went on forever. When I turned slightly to get my bearings, I fell backwards into the snow. There, to my right was a stream. How I had managed to miss it was beyond me. I couldn't believe I'd been running beside it this entire time and never once fell into it. I shivered at the thought of the freezing water. I'd always loved to look at water and appreciated its soothing effect, but as I looked at *this* stream, it appeared black and there was nothing soothing about that. I cautiously continued to walk along the water's edge, using it only as a guideline to stay on track.

I was still headed in the direction of the light in the distance, hoping it was leading me to a place where I could get warm. *Have faith, Novi.* The clouds shifted and moonlight once again lit my way. I looked up and smiled as I remembered the walking song from *The Lord of The Rings* my nanna used to sing to me. J.R.R. Tolkien was one of her favorite authors. I started to hum, careful to keep my voice low.

> *A day will come at last when I*
> *Shall take the hidden paths that run*
> *West of the Moon, East of the Sun.*

When the cloud cover cleared, illuminating the stream, I gasped. It was blood red and not stagnant as I assumed but flowing and alive. I swallowed hard. The images of the villagers, the smell of the burning wood, and the screaming—all of it played back in my head. I started to hum again, this time more shakily.

A day will come at last when I
Shall take the hidden paths that run
West of the Moon, East of the Sun.

"Nanna, what do I do? How can I fix this?" I said out loud as if someone was going to respond. Was this it, had I finally lost it?

I slogged through the drifts and shivered with each step. The moonlight was helping guide my way, but I was losing faith, and strength, that I would make it to a place where I could be safe and warm. I saw a bridge in the distance and convinced my mind this was a sign. *Maybe it's the way to get to Hortus.*

It took me some time, but I finally made it to the stone bridge. Something about it seemed familiar too—the Fairy Bridge? But how? My mind snapped. This was it. I was home. When all this started I was in Scotland, near my grandparents' house—near the Fairy Bridge. Hope surged. I walked faster. I was almost halfway across the bridge when the shrill sound of the Lunatishee rang out in the distance. *No!* My mind screamed. *No!*

I started to run but tripped and hit the stone railing. I lost my footing and fell. The freezing water surrounded me, and I began to sink. I should have fought my way to the surface, but my body and my mind had made a different choice. I was still lost in Sacrife and I was frozen. All the elements of me gave up. *The world would be better off without me anyway.* I was free floating, drifting further and further into the darkness, and I didn't care anymore about the consequences. The choice was made. *No more guilt. No more need for redemption from all the people I've let down. Besides, this is just giving into the inevitable. You're already gone anyway, I mean how else did you end up here in the land of make believe and fairies if you were still alive and well?*

I gave in to the weight around me. I'd become the Lady of the Lake without Excalibur, the damsel in distress without the prince to save her, Dorothy without her slippers or Alice without her "drink me" potion. Fantastic dreams weaved into amazing tales of triumph over obstacles. I was not triumphant over anything. I was a coward.

"Novi, come here. I want to read you a story," Nanna called out.

I scampered into the room where Nanna was. She loved her library, loved her books. She had everything from children's books to the classics. She read it all and cherished each one. Whenever my pappa was away on travel, he would find a rare book and bring it home to her as a present, and she would be overjoyed. Nanna had no need for fancy jewelry or extravagant gifts, all she wanted was to read something that transported her into another world. I think that's where I developed my love for reading. She lit a passion within me for the written word when I was a kid, and I haven't been able to stop the fire that burns within me since. It's just part of who I am.

I pulled down her copy of The Wonderful Wizard of Oz and ran my hands over the image of the cowardly lion. I remember when Pappa gave this to her. It was an anniversary gift for their fiftieth. You would've thought he gave her a twelve carat diamond. I slid the book carefully back into its slot and pulled down a copy of Alice in Wonderland. As I flipped through it, I smiled. Page after page I could hear Nanna's voice reading to me. I walked back into the living room and laid down. It had been quite some time since I read this book and with the chill in the air and the clouds overhead, now seemed like as good a time as any to stay in my pajamas and read.

"Who in the world am I? Ah, that's the great puzzle."

That quote, Novaleigh, will be one you will have to figure out on your own. That is your quest in this life—to figure out who you are and who you want to be. Your mom and I have aspirations for you but what we want most is for you to know who you are for yourself. Each of us has our own path to follow, someday you will see yours clearly.

"But I know my path now, Nanna."

"Oh you do, do you? And what is the path you wish to take?"

"I'm going to be a famous artist. Everyone will love my pictures as much as you do."

She smiled as I handed her my latest drawing. "You're right, my sweet girl, everyone will love them as much as I do."

I closed the book and stared up at the ceiling. I was five at the time and my art was less than polished, but Nanna made me feel like I could've been the next Van Gogh. I think the last time I picked up a pencil to draw anything I was fourteen. It was about the same time I gave up anything creative for other pursuits, aka boys. I chuckled remembering the first boy I ever kissed. It started out awkward and then turned into bliss. I thought I'd died and gone to heaven until his hands started to move up my shirt, and then I twisted his arm behind his back and dropped him to his knees—a trick my burly Scottish pappa taught me. From that moment on, I shifted my thoughts to books and the arts in general. Then I met Gavin and things were great. A boy to hang out with who also loved art and books, and we got along perfectly.

Gavin. *All of my thoughts eventually led back to Gavin.*

"He wasn't angry with me when I saw him at Nanna and Pappa's house, he was something else. No, Gavin hated you when you saved him from the warden," I argued with myself. "Which is true? It doesn't matter now. Now he will either mourn your loss or despise you even more for your weakness. Why are you so weak, Novaleigh? Why?"

Further into the abyss.

My body jerked and I was suddenly pulled upwards in a rush. I heard my name but it was faint and almost inaudible. Who was calling me? Why was I colder now? No, not colder—warmer but only in places where I was being touched. *Odd.*

Panic set in.

OH GOD! The warden. Lithia. The Lunatishee, they found me. Again, you foolish child, why does it matter? You made your choice. You have fallen.

"Novi! Can you hear me? Are you all right?"

"No, she is not all right! We have to get her out of here. We have to get her to Hortus now or she will die."

"She's so cold, Oliver."

"This is not working. I need to go to my burrow to get the proper medicine for her."

"And where is that?"

"A half days journey, one way, but I will try to be faster."

"Will she survive that long?"

"She will if we can level her body temperature."

"Then go. I will care for her until you return."

"I won't let you and Novi down, Gavin."

"I know you care for her. Please hurry."

"I will."

"One more thing, Oliver, can you make the fire bigger for us?"

Loud crackling sounds echoed in the distance. All of this was faint and foggy, but I heard two voices conversing even though it sounded as if it all took place underwater. *Ah, yet another dream.* How long does it take a person to die? Will I crossover or am I to remain in this limbo—stuck between two worlds?

"I've got you, Novi. Please don't leave me. I can't lose you again."

Gavin? No. Can't be. But all thoughts lead back to him— lead back to all your mistakes.

Peace. Blissful peace.

Chapter Sixteen

I got dressed and layered myself just in case the temperature dropped or it started to rain. Before I put on my wellies, I grabbed a blanket and Nanna's copy of The Velveteen Rabbit off the shelf before heading out the door. It was my favorite book she would read to me. The cover was as tattered as the velveteen rabbit himself, but just like him, it didn't matter at all because real *couldn't be ugly, except to people who didn't understand. I understood. The worn edges showed the love for each word, in not only repetition but in the voices who read it to me—Nanna, Mom, even Pappa when he wasn't busy. This story was rooted in my soul.*

'It doesn't happen all at once,' said the Skin Horse. 'You become. It takes a long time. That's why it doesn't happen often to people who break easily, or have sharp edges, or who have to be carefully kept.'

It's funny how the message of being authentic and vulnerable was part of becoming real and yet, for as much as I treasured this book, I failed to remember what was most important.

"There will be things that happen to you in life, Novi that will test your strength. Your job is to rise above the challenges and not be so fragile. You are a special little girl, Novi. Never forget that, but don't let your uniqueness cloud your vision," Nanna whispered. "Special means you give more than you take because that is where the true magic is revealed."

I wasn't special. My edges were too sharp, and I'd become someone who had to be carefully kept. My magic couldn't be revealed. I'm so sorry, Nanna.

Had there been lessons in other stories Nanna read to me? I made her read Beauty and the Beast at least a thousand times, too.

The sun was now high in the sky, but the breeze still carried a chill. I wrapped the blanket around myself and made my way down to the shoreline. It was so beautiful here. My grandparent's house was situated between the coastline and the cliffs, giving them the best of both worlds. I knelt down and scooped a handful of the cool, clear water into my hands and let it slip through my fingers. Peaceful was the only word I could use to describe how I was feeling. Despite the temperature of the water, my body felt warm and light.

I walked over to a clearing near some shady trees and laid out the blanket. The only place in New York to find something even remotely like this was Central Park, but it was too busy to be considered a place of respite. The fast paced life of the city had me constantly plugged into something, and it felt so normal to have something scheduled every hour of the day. Why are our lives so jam packed with events that we lose out on moments like this?

My stillness was merging with the air around me, and I felt calm for the first time in years. I didn't want to move for fear of breaking the spell it had me under. I just want to be like this forever. I am happy here with no one expecting anything from me. Here, I can live in the space between lost and happy without judgment of my emotional state. Here, I am just Novaleigh Darrow—a girl who loves to read and draw. A woman on the verge of a breakthrough of becoming who she was meant to be. A soul who wants to be loved by someone who can accept her true nature and not the persona she portrays to make sure people feel comfortable around her.

Tears spilled out of me as if I was being purged of all my pain. It felt so real, and I wanted desperately to believe that when I stood and walked away from this place I would feel redeemed, but I knew that was a pipe dream. The real world doesn't work that way. The real world wasn't a fantasy you could escape. No, the real world required sacrifice and compromise. Payment for a life travelled I supposed.

I wonder what the world would look like if I were its creator. Would there be suffering and joy in equal measure or would it just be joyful? No, there would have to be balance—a ying to the yang. It's the nature of all things, or so I've been told.

I let my mind drift some more to the moments that made me smile. Gavin and I the first day of me going to his school. It was funny to watch him interact with the other kids. He was such a clumsy, goofy nerd, and he was different than the rest of them. He spoke perfect English, which around here was unusual. Most of the people who lived in the Isle of Skye were Scotts through and through. Gavin was the guy all the other guys made fun of because he was so incredibly intelligent, and they couldn't keep up. And the girls, well, they were a different story. They'd all do double takes because he was tall with dark hair, and he had the most beautiful crystal green eyes. He was hot, but he was shy too, and that shyness left him vulnerable to caddy females. I'd overheard one of the girls saying to her gang of friends that they'd like to take him into the janitor's closet and kiss him until he turned stupid. It was such an odd thing to say. Little did they know, the joke would be on them. Gavin was a helluva kisser.

"Hey."

"Hey. How's the first day going?"

"Charming," I said as I grinned. "Interesting girls here at this school."

"Yeah, they all act stuck up, but I'm sure you'll find someone to hang out with soon enough."

"Maybe, but I already have a friend, and I'm not really taking applications for new ones."

"You're so weird."

"And don't you forget it."

After that, Gavin and I were inseparable. His father was friends with my Pappa, and it just so happened that Gavin would always accompany him whenever he visited. His parents were divorced too. His mom was from London and when she and Gavin's dad decided to call it quits, she went back home. That explained why he spoke without the typical Scottish brogue

"Novi. Please wake up."

"I can't. I'm too tired."

"But you're talking to me."

"Noooooo," I dragged out. "I've fallen. I am lost."

"We saved you. You are here with me. Open your eyes and see."

I thought for a moment about what it would be like to see him again but knew in my heart he'd only be a mirage like the light in the distance I was chasing. I squeezed my eyes tighter. "No, I cannot be fooled."

He laughed. "You've done that since we were kids, and I've never understood why. Do you think by squeezing your eyes tight that you're changing the channel on what's before you?"

My eyes flew open. "Gavin. You're here?"

He nodded his head but only slightly because he was holding me tight. Our bodies were joined, skin to skin, as we lay in front of a roaring fire. "What…"

"Be still. Your body is ice cold, and this is the only way to help bring your temperature back to normal. Oliver is fetching medicine for you."

I sighed contentedly. "Okay."

"No resistance, eh?"

"Too tired. Besides, I'd dreamed of this moment too many times to wish it were untrue. I want to be here in your arms."

Gavin's heart began to race. I could hear it clearly since my head was resting on his chest. "Why does this surprise you? You know how much I love you."

His breath hitched. "Actually. No, I don't."

I looked up at him lazily. "I think I have loved you since the first time we made out in the barn, and I never stopped."

"But you left me, Novi. You told me you needed more in your life besides a relationship. Correction. I heard from your nanna that you needed more because you were too much of a coward to tell me yourself."

There wasn't any anger in his voice like there was when I said goodbye to him in Cadent. No, this was more sadness and grief.

"You're right. I was a coward and a fool. You were…no are…my best friend. The one I want to tell everything to, but I was too stupid to see all of that. Too selfish. You are my biggest regret, and if I could go back to that moment and change it, I would." I closed my eyes again and rested my head back on his bare chest.

"I don't know what to say to that, Novi."

"I don't expect you to say anything. I screwed up, and now I'm dying. The best I can hope for is that before I pass you can forgive me. I never meant to hurt you, and I know I did. I hurt us both."

Gavin lifted my chin so our eyes could meet. "You are not dying. I won't allow it."

I gave him a sad smile. "It's too late."

"It's never too late," he said as his lips touched mine. "I love you, too. I always have."

Our kiss deepened, and warmth began to spread over my body. Was this real? Was Gavin really kissing me? Had he really just said he loved me too and always had? Wait, I said that. *Novaleigh you have become a trickster. You're mind so splintered and fractured that fantasy and reality are intertwined into an intricate web of wants and desires with no truth to connect them.*

My body burned for his touch. I wanted us to be together the way we used to. I needed his caress until my body was his in every way. Chills ran over me as his hand slid down between us, finding the spot he loved best. For being the nerdy boy growing up, he always knew the perfect way to bring me to climax—every time and with minimal effort, too. All those high school girls who dismissed him because they couldn't see past his goofy quirkiness would never know how much of an amazing and giving lover he was. *Their loss.* Gavin was a hot, sexy nerd. The best kind.

A moan escaped my body as he continued to let his fingers delve in and out of me. "Gods I've missed you, Novi," he breathed into my mouth as he broke our kiss.

"Is this real? Am I dreaming?"

"This is not a dream."

"Thank god, because I need you, Gavin." I let my hand run down his chest, until I felt him hard against my hand. Gavin groaned as I let my fingers trail the length of him.

"I want to be inside you, Novi."

Dream or no, I wanted that too. If I was dying and this was the last thing I'd experience, then he and I together would be the one thing I wanted before I found my peace.

I moved on top of him and he slid inside, gentle at first, but as the intensity of our movements increased, our bodies melded together in perfect unison. We moved as one as if no time had passed between us. Our love and connection was in every kiss, every move of my hips. All we needed was one another. Our passion built into an intoxicating mixture of lust and devotion. Ever since our first time, we were bound to one another, mind, body, and soul. I was the only thing that broke that connection. In this moment, I believed that maybe redemption was possible. Gavin had seen the ugly in me and loved me in spite of it. Maybe it wasn't too late for me—for us.

We both cried out as we found our release and remained motionless for a few moments until the waves of passion subsided. I didn't want to move, didn't want this perfect dream to end.

Gavin kissed me gently as I moved to lay beside him. I once again curled into his arms, a seamless fit, and closed my eyes. I could die now.

"I will love you always, Gavin. Always," I said sleepily.

He hugged me tighter and mumbled into my hair. "Always is a very long time. You sure you can promise that, Novi?"

I looked up at him. "I can now."

Chapter Seventeen

I was so tired, my mind drifting from alert to asleep as I lay in Gavin's arms.

"Wake up, Novi," he said as he ran his hands up and down my arms, warming them with the friction. "Stay with me."

"I'm awake," I slurred.

"Then open your eyes and look at me."

As I opened my eyes, Gavin smiled. He, however, was not the only thing to catch my eye. The sky behind him was varying shades of orange, pink, and purple. "Where are we? Where is all the snow?" I tried to move but Gavin held me close.

"It's all right. You're safe."

"Where is The White?" My hands started to shake and my voice trembled. "The warden? Lithia?"

"Shhh, shhh, shhh. You're safe. I told you. Oliver and I saved you. You fell into the water below the bridge and we pulled you out—brought you here."

"To where?" I looked around hesitantly.

"We're just inside the boundary of Hortus. Oliver said we would be safe here until he returned."

"Not safe. We are not safe. I thought I was safe with the elven fae but they're all gone—dead because of me."

"Novi, that wasn't your fault. The Lunatishee killed them, not you."

"If I had not been in their village, they would still be alive," I cried.

"Novi, I need you to focus on you getting well. You almost died."

"I did die." Tears streamed down my face. "Where is Oliver?"

"He had to go to his burrow to get you some medicine." *Medicine?* My mind was swimming. I already knew where Oliver had gone, but then again, did I? I'd heard it in my dream, but now that Gavin was saying it, it seemed real.

"I don't understand, Gavin."

"You've been out of it, Novi. Wavering between conscious and unconscious. You were half frozen and we tried everything to revive you. Oliver even used the crystal you had around your neck, but nothing was working. He said he knew of something that would help but it was at his home and that he'd be back soon."

I reached for the crystal around my neck and indeed found it gone. I then looked down between Gavin and me, only to realize we were naked. Gavin blushed. "Sorry, it was the only way I knew how to warm you up. You know—body heat."

My face suddenly felt hot. "So you and I, that wasn't a dream?"

He shook his head no.

"And you and I—all that we talked about last night—that really happened?"

He kissed me. One peck and then another. "It really happened," he said as his hands caressed my cheek. "I don't want to ever be without you again."

I sobbed into his next kiss. "I'm so sorry for everything. I made so many mistakes, and I know I'll never be able to make up for them, but if you'll let me, I'd like to spend the rest of my days trying."

He didn't respond with words.

Our bodies were once again intertwined, except this time I was remembering it all. Each touch, every kiss, the feel of his hands as they roamed over my body—mine over his. I was mentally recording every single second of us together. Not that I needed to, since it seems Gavin and I were on the same page about starting over, but just in case I was still dreaming, I focused on every delicious detail.

I don't know how long Gavin and I enjoyed being lost in one another, but as the sun kissed the tops of the great trees I was feeling a bit better even though my skin felt hot. *You just had sex...duh.*

I moved to get up, but Gavin wouldn't let me walk around. He said that I may be coherent and more alert, but my skin was still too white for his comfort level. And with all we'd just done, he wanted to wait until Oliver gave me his medicine before he'd be totally confident I was well enough to be up and around.

A rustling in the distance startled us both, and Gavin moved to shield me from whatever it was. The bushes at the foot of the trees separated and out came Oliver carrying an extra-large satchel over his shoulder. *Good grief, how much medicine did I need?* Gavin covered me so none of my flesh was showing as Oliver drew closer.

Oliver looked at us both skeptically. "What is this?" he demanded.

"You told me we needed to get her temperature up. This is how humans do that," Gavin replied.

"I see." Oliver dropped the bag over his shoulder and let it hit to the ground with a thud. "Well, you are alone no longer. Please put on some garments so I may be around you both," he huffed.

Oliver turned around, and Gavin moved to put on his pants and a shirt that he'd been using to rest his head on. It was covered in a bit of dirt and leaves, but he didn't seem to care. "Oliver?" Gavin paused. "Novi's clothes were ruined. Between the battle she endured and almost drowning, well, she doesn't have anything to wear."

Oliver didn't turn, instead just slipped the knot on the bag and pulled out a pale green dress. He handed it over his shoulder to Gavin. "This should do for now. When we get to the village in Hortus, Freylar, can make her a garment of her choosing."

"Thank you, Oliver," I said as Gavin handed the dress to me. "I appreciate you bringing it to me and for saving me." Oliver crossed his arms in front of his chest, still with his back facing me. "I'm serious. I know I've been nothing but trouble to you since I've arrived."

I pulled the dress over my head and walked over to Oliver and hugged him tightly from behind, kissing his furry face until he was pushing me away. "All right, all right. I get it. You're grateful."

I swayed a bit and Gavin caught me, lowering me gently back to the makeshift bedding.

"See, I told you weren't ready to be up and around."

Gavin felt my head and turned to give Oliver a poignant look. "She's hot."

Oliver rushed to my other side and unwrapped a woven bag. "Novaleigh, I am going to give you some medicine. It is an ancient remedy handed down from my mother's side. It's always been tried and true."

"What's wrong with me?"

"You have a fever, Novaleigh. We need to get it down. You survived The White, but its effects have taken a toll on your body. This is a mixture of herbs in combination with a clear quartz."

As Oliver used the crystal point to crush the herbs in an iridescent shell, I closed my eyes. I could smell cinnamon and bay leaves. They were scents I knew, but I don't think I'd ever smelled them mixed together. They did, however, remind me of my nanna's cooking.

"How will this mixture help, Oliver? It smells like something I should be putting in a stew."

He shook his head and laughed. "Is she always like this, Gavin?"

"Yes. She finds humor in lots of normal everyday boring things."

"Hey," I said as I smacked him on the shoulder.

"No, it's cute."

Oliver looked between the two of us. "So when did you two come to terms?"

"Just recently." I blushed.

Oliver nodded. "I see."

"Is that a bad thing?" Gavin asked.

"No, it's about time actually," he said as he finished wrapping the crystal. "Everyone but you two could see it."

"See what?" I played stupid.

"The love between you," Oliver said with a raised brow. "I know you know it. Both of you."

"I guess it takes almost losing someone to realize what you have," Gavin admitted.

"Well, I hope you two have realized how stupid that is. Waiting until something terrible happens to decide to face your truth is only punishing yourself. If you lost one another, the pain would be far worse than the guilt or pride you were feeling by staying apart, would it not?"

I pursed my lips. What could I say to that? Oliver was right. I should've told Gavin a long time ago how I really felt— owned up to everything. Instead, we lost years apart because I was too obstinate. Since I arrived in Sacrife, I didn't understand why, but now I'm beginning to understand. I hit rock bottom and the only place I can go now is up, but only if I choose it.

My body felt odd. I was so hot. Sweat was beading on my forehead and my teeth started to chatter. Panic set it and Oliver reached for my hand. "It's part of the process, Novi. When you wake in the morning you'll be better."

"But it's morning now," I said between breaths.

"I know and I'm sorry. The medicine will take some time to work, Novi. The cinnamon will begin to heat you from the inside and the bay leaf will help to purge your body of the fever. It's the only way to get you beyond The White's sickness."

Gavin moved so he could hold me. "And what does the crystal do? The last one didn't work."

"It amplifies everything around it. Just make sure to keep it on her forehead. It will draw on all the other elements within and heal her from the inside out," Oliver sighed. "And the other crystal did work, Gavin. When it exploded, it created a dome around you both, shielding you from the outside. The moonlight charged it to keep you hidden by everyone other than those who hold favor with the queens."

"But I never held favor with them," Gavin said as he held my quivering hands.

Oliver smiled. "You did the moment you chose to save Novaleigh over yourself. Una and Uphren bound you to Novi with that act."

"Oh, God." I stuttered. "So. If. I. Die. He will. Too?"

"No, not that kind of bound. You two have never known it, but you are twin flames. Your love is timeless and beyond all realms and worlds. Blessed by the Great Mother herself." Oliver smiled. "You both showing up here was no accident. You are two pieces of the same whole—one negative and one positive. Energy constantly flowing between you."

"I don't understand," Gavin admitted.

"Have you ever felt her pain or happiness even when you were apart?"

Gavin looked down at me. "Yes. Even now."

"And what about you, Novaleigh?"

I nodded wearily.

"You two rest. I will keep watch," Oliver said as he took the moss blanket and laid it over us. "You will need to, now more than ever, draw on one another for strength. We still have hurdles to climb before we are able to breathe easy."

"Thank you, Oliver," Gavin replied.

Oliver smiled but didn't respond. Instead he walked over to the extra-large satchel and pulled out a quiver full of arrows and flung them over his shoulder. I wanted to ask what he needed them for, but my eyelids grew heavy, and in moments I was asleep.

Chapter Eighteen

I woke in a rush, the same way I had the night the elven village was attacked. *Why am I always asleep when things are happening around me?* There was screaming and again heat—as if my skin was on fire—*Oh God!* I sat up and called out for Gavin and Oliver but there was no answer, only the loud screeching sound that accompanied the Lunatishee. I flipped off the blanket and ran around hoping to find them, but nothing. I was alone. Had they left me? Worse?

My heart was racing as I ran into the darkness. *Oh no, it's nighttime and I wasn't supposed to wake until the morning with Oliver's medicine. What went wrong?* I tripped over a log and stumbled on the ground, trying to gain my footing so I could run again, but instead I felt moisture on my feet. My toes were tipping the edge of an embankment, and I froze in place. It wasn't cold like the stream in The White, instead it felt warm like bath water. I strained my eyes and gasped when a ray of moonlight shone from the pitch of the night.

The water was not water at all, it was blood red. Just like the one I'd seen in The White. My body was shaking as I tried to step back but ran into something hard.

"You didn't think you could escape us that easily, did you?" a deep menacing voice taunted in my ear. "I told you that you were the one I was looking for." The warden ran his hands through my hair but then yanked it to wrench my neck backwards. I cried out and he laughed. "Weakness. It's what you are."

Tears were streaming down my face as I tried to tamp down the fear clouding all rational thought. "What do you want? Why me?"

"Why do you ask such stupid questions? You are selfish and have let down so many people. You must be punished."

"What?" my voice quivered.

He pulled my hair tighter. "How many more bodies are you going to leave in your wake? The poor fool bound in the water, I don't know exactly what you did to him, but his pain was palpable and I never laid a hand on him. Then there was the seer, you didn't even try to save her. No, you just let her suffer. And my favorite," he droned, "you killed an entire village of innocent fae because you were too busy trying to save yourself."

I shook my head. "No. That's not true," I cried.

"The verdict—selfish. The punishment—death."

"I don't want to die."

"Don't you?"

"No!"

"Your dreams. Your actions. You don't value life or the important things that matter because if you did, we wouldn't be here."

Lithia appeared before me and gripped my throat. "Finally. I have been so hungry since you managed to get away. I'm practically starved," she said with a menacing grin, "and you will be a perfect meal."

I tried to speak but between the grip the warden had on my hair and the chokehold Lithia had on my throat, I was fading. What had she meant, '*I would be a perfect meal*'? What the hell was happening? Where were Oliver and Gavin?

As if on cue, Lithia laughed. "I can see you trying to figure this out so let me make it easy for you. No one is coming to save you. You fell. You landed here in Sacrife, had a chance at redemption but failed. Now you are mine." She released my throat and ran a long claw-like nail down my cheek, drawing blood. She licked the blood and moaned. "So much sweeter than I assumed. I may need to savor this. Warden, care for a taste?"

"I did find redemption," I croaked. "I made my peace, and death or no death, I have that." With what energy I had left, I wrenched out of the warden's grasp and pushed Lithia backwards. "What have you done to Gavin and Oliver?" I screamed.

A thunderous roar echoed from the heavens and ripped through the air. Something was overhead and it was massive by the sound of it. In a blinding flash, the sky lit up and we were no longer bathed in darkness. Instead, the horizon was suffused with ombre shades of purple and green. At first glance it almost looked like an overexposed image of the aurora borealis. There, in the sky, was a black and grey wolf the size of a dragon. *This is it. The final smidgen of my mind has cracked. A wolf with wings, snarling and growling? I'VE LOST MY DAMN MIND!*

Lithia hissed and the warden unsheathed a bulky dagger from his hip, readying himself for battle.

"What is that?" I mumbled under my breath.

"Do not move," Lithia fumed as she gripped my wrist.

"Why is she here?" the warden snapped.

As the wolf flew overhead, I saw the faint wisp of someone riding it—flashes of white and bits of pink. *The queens? No, there was only one. Who could this be?* The divide between The White and Hortus had become visible in the illuminated sky as the wolf shifted and looked for a clearing. The frozen tundra and the bright cheer of spring clashed as they were juxtaposed to one another. Finally, the great beast found a spot and landed with a thud in the snow. He bowed to let the person riding dismount and growled one last time, turning his head towards the three of us. It was like a warning, but I doubted the person standing next to him needed the backup, since Lithia and the warden seemed on edge with their arrival.

When the person stepped into the snow, I knew it was a woman, but I still was clueless as to who it could be. She walked slowly towards the three of us with no fear in her eyes or her walk. She held a tall stick in her right hand, and it made a sharp tinking sound with each step she took. The closer she got, I was able to see what was making the noise. The staff was covered in keys of all shapes and sizes. They were ornate and frozen, which I assumed was part of the unnerving sound it made as the metals clanged against one another.

The woman stood before us now, only a few feet away, and I was taken aback. She was the most beautiful woman I'd ever seen. Even more beautiful than the twin queens when I met them. Her face was stark white, like Lithia's, but her cheeks and hair were tinted pink. The woman was wearing a dress made of frosted pink roses. Was she frozen? Partially thawed? *I'm losing it.*

When Lithia went to speak, the half frozen woman, thrust her staff into the air and slammed it into the ground. Shattering the ice and melting it instantly. The warmth began to spread outwards from her as she glared at Lithia. "If you are going to address me, you will do it properly, and if you do not call off your dog," she said with a side glance to the warden, "I will remind you of exactly who I am and what I can do."

The warden snarled and moved in a way that startled me. I dropped to my knees, hoping to avoid the bloodshed I was certain would follow. Lithia and the warden called out for the Lunatishee to attack and all hell broke loose.

Out of the trees came two Lunatishee who appeared to have doubled in size from the ones I saw back in The White. They were enormous and hurling their poisonous spikes at the dragon sized wolf, but they were no match for him. He whipped one with this tail, flinging it back into the trees and the other one he ripped apart with his teeth. When he was done, he licked his massive paws as if nothing had just happened. I was dumbstruck. The beautiful woman never flinched, instead she glared at the two before her as if pondering her next move.

The warden lunged at the woman but was gone in a flash. The woman simply snapped her fingers and he was obliterated. Ashes dissipated, leaving nothing but that putrid yellow smoke lingering in the air.

"Nooooo," Lithia screamed.

"I warned you, Lithia. As I have warned you most of your life. Your ambition exceeds your ability."

"You always say that, Mother, and you are always wrong!"

Mother?

"I'm never wrong."

"I want her," Lithia whined as she pointed to me.

"She is not yours to have."

"But she is. She came to me."

"No I didn't!" I took a chance and screamed.

"Yes. You. Did," she raged. "You came to Sacrife with your pain and anger. My sisters may have tried to cover your angst with pastel colors and promises of peace, but what you really want is to be swallowed by your darkness. I tasted it. Your blood is sweet with pain and misery. You want to wallow in the loss of all the things you should have, could have, would have done. You are a weak fool who needs me. I'm the best part of you, Novaleigh," she said as she spat my name in disgust.

"How could you be the best part of me? You're miserable. You want others to hurt and be as pitiful as you. I want nothing to do with you."

She smirked. "That's the beauty of me. I live in the shadows waiting for my moment. You visit, whisper your deepest secrets and I wait. *'I don't want to live anymore like this. I can't continue to feel this empty inside. I want to fall into a dream and never come back. Here I feel nothing but pain, maybe if I was gone I could be free.'* Do you remember those words, Novaleigh? Do you remember your wretched dream?"

I stood there, silent. Those had been my thoughts. My darkest thoughts. The moments I keep to myself for fear others would judge me. I was in a dark place after my grandparents died. I lost them—lost everyone that mattered to me. I lost Gavin but most importantly, I lost myself. Gavin was the one I wanted to turn to when my heart was breaking, but I'd left him—dismissed him for something more. Who could I turn to? Ethan was vapid. He only cared for himself, and I didn't want to burden my parents with my problems. After their divorce, I was left reeling. Why, I don't know. They're problems had nothing to do with me. I was not the reason their marriage failed. They still loved me. I knew that with every fiber of my being. They just didn't love each other.

Gavin loved me, and I was scared, scared I'd be lost in him and forget me, so I ran as far away as I could. I had no idea when I made that choice that I'd only hurt myself. And now, with Nanna and Pappa gone, hope for the fairytale seemed like a dream, so I made it one. I went there as often as I could to feel what I was incapable of feeling in the real world. In my dream, I could be whomever I wanted to be, do magical things and say the words I should've said when I had the chance. My dream was my solace.

"There she goes again," Lithia sang out. "See I told you, Mother. Lost in her thoughts until she drowns in them. Like I said, you came to me, Novaleigh, not the other way around."

I shook my head. "No," I repeated over and over again, hoping it wasn't true, but Lithia was right. I did get lost in my dark thoughts until they were all I could think about.

"Tell Mother how you got here. Tell her about how you fell."

"I don't want to," I cried. "I am not proud of letting those thoughts rule my mind. I don't want anything to do with you, Lithia. I never meant for any of it to come true."

"But your thoughts have power, and that power shifted into focus until you fell," Lithia laughed. "You're mine now," she said as she reached for me.

"Not so fast, Lithia," the woman said in warning. "She may have fallen into Sacrife by choice initially, but now she has a chance to make a different one. What is your desire now, Novaleigh?"

My hands shook, but I wasn't sure what was causing it. Anger at my secrets being exposed, fear of the truth, or the fact that I was indeed weak? I wanted to look at the woman and ask her how this was all possible and why did it matter what I desired now, but instead I just looked at the ground. I may have dreamed this dream a thousand times, but now that I was here, I wanted to go home. I wanted something more. The conversation with Gavin. The talking otters, the fairies, and the elven village—all of it was apparently just me fabricating stories in my mind. I wasn't dreaming. Based on what Lithia said, I was dying—but by choice at that. I was weak. I didn't deserve another chance.

"Novaleigh?" the woman asked. "Whatever you are telling yourself, don't listen. Your mind can play tricks on you, or in this case my daughter can. She is the part of you that you wish to hide, and when you give her a voice with your thoughts, she can drown you with them." Lithia began to laugh, but quickly fell silent. I looked up and saw her mouth stitched with black threads. She looked like something out of a horror movie. "Her voice is now silenced. What do you want? What is your heart telling you, not your mind?"

"I want to live. I want to make better choices, follow my heart and do things that are spontaneous and adventurous," I blurted. "I want to tell Gavin I love him and that we were meant to be together in spite of everything between us. I want to live."

The woman smiled. "Good choice. One Una and Uphren knew you'd choose in the end. Oliver has guided you well, and I am pleased."

"This is all real?"

She nodded. "Once you come to the place where you can silence your inner demons. You can make the right choices. You can be free to live. You just have to choose it. You have to want it more than you want the sorrow."

"You mean Lithia is the embodiment of my pain?"

169

"In a way, yes."

"But I thought white meant purity and peacefulness. There is nothing about her that is peaceful," I replied as I looked at Lithia who was ripping at the stitches that bound her mouth shut.

"You're right in a way. White represents both a positive and negative aspect of all the colors. Just as you are light and dark, so is she. Her darkness, however, is ingrained into who she is. She chooses to express herself as someone innocent when she is far from it. Say the word and you can seal her fate."

"I don't want to kill her."

"I don't want you to kill her either. I do, however, want you to silence her."

"Haven't you already done that?" I said as I looked back over at Lithia.

"Close your eyes and decide to let her go, Novaleigh. Only you can quiet her. The darkness inside of you will never die, but with enough light you can keep her and your demons where they belong—buried." She smiled. "The trick will be to find the place where they can't bury you."

I looked at her skeptically. "Who are you? How do I know that you aren't another trick in my mind? I am a little unsure of people these days. Things in my mind have been really *off* lately."

"I am the Great Mother and you don't have to doubt me. I am no trick."

"But…"

"Lithia told you she brought you here, but that was a lie. I brought you here so you could grow and change. You said you wanted to live. Was that true?"

"Well, yes," I stammered.

"Then send her away and choose to live."

Tears streamed down my face. I had no idea how to truly silence her, or them, or whatever this was, but I did want to start again. I clenched my fists and closed my eyes. I thought about all the things that had happened here in Sacrife and wished it all was just a really bad dream and that when I woke up, I would be home, safe and sound. I also wished that when I woke, I'd find Gavin and we'd talk and I could explain to him as I had explained to Gavin here all the things I wish I'd done differently. I would make this right. I opened my eyes and watched as Lithia dissipated just as the warden had, into a haze of dust. The only difference was that hers exploded into shades of grey. A perfect blend of the dark and light.

"Is she gone?" I asked.

"Most of her but not in the way you're assuming. Her essence is what dissipated, but she is still alive. It will take some time for her to pull herself together, but once she does, she'll be back to her old tricks," the Great Mother explained. "I'm curious though, what did you do to make her leave?"

"I asked for this all to be a dream."

"I see."

"Was that not enough?"

"No, there is another part to the puzzle you have to figure out before you can go home," she said as she took my hand in hers, "and Novaleigh, this is not a dream."

Chapter Nineteen

The sky was clear and The White seemed far off in the distance as I looked out at the great beast. He was sitting very still, so much so, he almost looked like a statue. The Great Mother waved her staff and the large wolf tucked his wings and moved in our direction. He was growing smaller with each step he took and would stop every little bit to shake off the snow from his fur. By the time he reached her side, he was the size of large puppy. He looked up at her with affection, and she bent down to dust off the last clump of snow that rested on the top of his head.

"This is Rafe."

"Hello?" I replied in a shaky voice. "How...how did he just..."

The Great Mother smiled. "Rafe is a chimera. He's my baby and my protector," she said as she picked him up to pet him. "You're safe with him as long as you are in my favor."

"Then I promise to stay in your good graces. I've seen his other side," I blurted.

"Are you ready to go?"

"Um, pardon my rudeness, but can we go back to the part where I should be waking up and moving on and this is not a dream."

"Sure," she said as she stroked Rafe's fur, "Can we walk and talk though? We need to meet up with Oliver and Gavin a bit up the road."

"They're alive?"

"Of course. Why would you think otherwise?"

"The blood in the stream. There was so much of it."

"Nothing but a trick of the mind Lithia's pet used to scare his prey."

"Effective trick," I quipped. "Did you kill the warden?"

"Yes," she said flatly. "He did more harm than good, and there is no room in my world for people who want to torture others for their own pleasure. Pain and heartache are natural byproducts of life, Novaleigh, but they shouldn't be a staple.

We're all better off here without him. Have you ever had someone like that in your life?"

I sniggered. "Yeah, a few actually."

"So then you know letting go of things that don't suit you or move you forward is freeing, yes?"

I smiled. "Absolutely."

"Can you think of other things you should let go of?" she probed.

I gave her an incredulous look. "But I did. I opened my heart to Gavin and told him everything. He forgave me and we were in a good place before the fever set in."

"Ah yes, the healing herbs Oliver used worked well. You are much improved."

I stopped mid-step. "Why am I still here though? I thought if..."

"You and Gavin worked things out and you wished away Lithia and the darkness, but you have yet to complete the most important part."

"Which is?"

"You have to forgive yourself. Until you can do that, you will remain here with us."

I shook my head and moved to follow. I wanted to be done with this, but I guess I was nowhere close to the end of this insanity. As we walked, the Great Mother's dress changed. She went from being the icy white queen, with keys jingling and partially frozen flowers covering her dress, to a warm and cheerful persona. Her dress was now shades of green and muted yellows. She looked like a vision of spring—a tree in bloom after months of hibernation—her hair now a vibrant auburn and her eyes the most beautiful shade of hazel.

"Can you change into anything?"

"Yes." She smiled. "So can you."

"Yeah, right."

"It's true. Your thoughts carry energy and power. Try it." I looked at her like she was mad. "Change my look simply by thinking it? Sure."

"Are you always this skeptical?" she asked.

I nodded my head.

"Trust and faith, Novaleigh. I'd advise you learn how to accept these things more freely, or I will be telling Oliver to build you a treehouse because you'll be staying awhile."

My eyes went wide. "Fine. How do I start?"

"Close your eyes and think about what you'd like to change. Focus your thoughts on it and breathe."

I closed my eyes and slowed my breathing, but I couldn't focus my thoughts. What would I change? My hair was still pink from when the twin queens changed it and while it was cool, it wasn't me. Maybe purple? I loved the color purple. I could go back to blonde, or I could go dark. I never had the guts to dye my hair black. I was always afraid of what people would think. I opened one eye to look at the Great Mother.

"Anything change?"

She laughed. "Are you going to pick one of those or stick with all three?"

"What?"

She pointed to the stream and I ran to look. I stared at my reflection. The top was a soft lavender that blended into a golden blonde and ended with tips of black. It was awful. I looked like a bizarre version of Neapolitan ice cream. I closed my eyes again and picked my favorite. When I opened my eyes, there it was, exactly as I wanted it. Soft curls fell at my shoulder and the black hue shimmered with hints of blue. My hair looked like a raven's feather.

"Beautiful choice," she complimented.

I beamed. "You don't think it's too dark?"

"I think if it's what your heart desires then it is perfect."

I twirled the end of one of the locks. "Thank you."

"Now are you ready to go?" she asked as she set Rafe back down on the ground.

"Yes."

Rafe looked up at us briefly, waited for an acknowledgement, and then ran off ahead of us, barking and scampering along as he played with the small woodland creatures he encountered along the way.

"Are we going to Hortus?"

"Yes, it'll be the place where you come to terms with all you've been struggling with. I think you'll really like it there."

I nodded. I'd liked every place I'd visited except for The White, but honestly, at this point, I couldn't see how another village was going to change my thoughts and bring me any closer to going home, but I had to try. Besides, I was enjoying spending time with the Great Mother, there was something very calming about being in her presence.

"Can I ask you something?"

"Of course," she replied kindly.

"Is your name *Great Mother*?"

"To most, but to others my name is Beira" she said as the corner of her mouth lifted. "It's not often, though, that people use my given name."

"May I call you, Beira?"

"I'd like that."

"Will you call me Novi? It's what all my friends call me, and I think I'd really like it if you did too."

Beira's smile widened. "Novaleigh is a beautiful name. Why do you wish to shorten it?"

"Because sometimes I don't feel like I live up to its potential, and Novaleigh is a mouthful." I laughed as we continued on the trail.

"First skeptical and now self-deprecating, why do you do this to yourself?"

I shrugged my shoulders. "I don't know. I just do. I have all the confidence in the world about some things, but then on others, I just...don't."

"You shouldn't doubt yourself. You have many talents and such wonderful gifts to share. The things you think are bad, others find endearing."

"I guess."

"So why do you feel as though you don't live up to your potential, Novi?"

"I was named partially from the word supernova and my nanna's middle name. My mom and Nanna were super close so they combined the names and voila," I said flippantly. "I haven't really lived up to my 'rare celestial phenomenon namesake,'" I air quoted.

"Have you tried?"

I went to reply but stopped. Had I tried? I'd followed what I thought was my path, and it ended up as a dead end. Not just a dead end but one that spiraled into a vortex of crazy. I landed here, in a land of make believe, since I was incapable of making my life what I wanted it to be, I created one—in my mind.

"I told you, Novi. This is not a dream."

My mouth dropped open. "I didn't say that out loud."

"You didn't have to," Beira replied. "I can hear your thoughts."

My lip started to quiver. Once again I felt like I was falling apart. Open and raw for all to see.

"Novi," a voice beckoned off in the distance. "Thank god you're safe."

Gavin and Oliver were running towards Beira and me, Gavin at a faster clip and making a beeline right in my direction. When he reached me, he picked me up and kissed me breathless.

"Please don't ever scare me like that again. I've lost you twice now. I can't lose you anymore." He kissed me again, long and intimate, as if no one else was around, but everyone was around—staring. Gavin set me down and looked at Beira and Oliver. "Sorry," he said unabashedly.

Oliver and Beira grinned before turning to walk ahead of us. Rafe came barking past, acting like a puppy.

"Cute dog," Gavin said as he ran between us.

"That's no dog," I said half aloud.

Chapter Twenty

Gavin intertwined our fingers as we walked, ignoring my comment about Rafe. Maybe he already knew. "Gavin. Where were you? I tried to find you and Oliver, but you were both gone. Did you leave me?"

Gavin stopped and pulled me to him. "No. I would never have left you. Oliver either. We were taken by these freaky looking clown characters and bound to some trees. I could hear you calling for us, but our mouths were covered and our hands and feet bound. We were helpless to do anything."

"How did you get free?"

"Fae warriors from Hortus. They found us and brought us back here. We tried to go after you but were told the Great Mother had you and you would be along soon."

I hugged him tighter. "She saved me."

"I'm grateful," he said as he kissed me again.

"Gavin," I said between kisses. "I'm sorry I brought you here. I didn't mean to."

"What are you talking about?"

"I didn't mean to bring you here to Sacrife—you're here because of me. You were taken because of me." Tears began to slide down my cheeks. "Beira said that until I can make peace with myself, I...I mean we, are stuck here."

Gavin gripped my chin and lifted it so we were face to face. "I don't care, Novi. As long as I am here with you, I don't care where we are."

"I love you, you know that right?"

"For a long time I thought you didn't, but I now know you do. I know you're sorry and for me what's in the past in just that, in the past. From this moment forward, we are together. Whatever we encounter we will encounter it together. Forgive yourself, Novi. I already have."

I bit down hard on my inner lip and tried to refrain from losing it. Beira had said the same thing. Why is it that everyone keeps telling me to forgive myself? How can I forgive myself for something I cannot make up for?

"Novi? What's wrong?"

"Nothing," I said as I wiped my eyes. "Maybe we should go."

"Sure," Gavin replied as he held my hand again. He squeezed it once, hard. His way of letting me know he would give me the space I needed to talk to him in time. Gavin knew me better than anyone; he knew if I was avoiding my feelings, I needed time to process them before I would talk about them. It was just my way. Thankfully, Gavin understood that. "It's getting dark and I'm hungry. These fae really know how to cook."

I chuckled. "I could eat."

Gavin reached for a lock of my hair. "What happened to the pink?" He grinned.

"Beira taught me how to change it?" I replied reluctantly.

"I like it. Dark and mysterious. It's sexy."

"Really?"

"Yeah, like, I want to take you behind those trees over there, sexy," he teased.

I smacked him on the shoulder. "Oh stop."

"Hey, I'm just being honest."

We strolled hand in hand through the forest with a comfortable ease between us. It was like it used to be, no tension, just two people who truly loved being with one another. As we continued on, I shifted my focus from Gavin and me to our location. Hortus was not hidden like Cadent and I wondered why, but Beira and Oliver had moved out of our view so I couldn't pose the question. Was it unique to the other places or had we already crossed through the portal and were now within the hidden boundaries?

Gavin and I walked until we were greeted by the most unusual looking fae—scantily clad females were adorned in gold chains, while a mossy-like material covered up only bits and pieces of their pale skin. The males were sleek and slender, their shirtless torsos heavily tattooed and marked with silver symbols. They were beautiful in their natural state and unashamed of their bodies. A fae woman walked by and was unlike the others. She had horns, but I couldn't tell at first glance if they were part of her or if they belonged to a headdress, because along with the horns there was a mass of feathers and tree bark. She was stunningly beautiful and was wearing more gold than the previous women I'd seen pass by. I wished Oliver was here so I could pepper him with questions. I bet he knew each one of these fae by name.

We followed the smell and found ourselves in a large dome shaped building. It looked like a great hall, with tables and chairs spread all around. There were lanterns hanging from the ceiling and two ornate wooden thrones positioned at the very front of the room. Fae were bustling about with food and drink, none of them seemed to be concerned by my and Gavin's appearance into their dining hall. Suddenly, everyone froze and bowed. From behind the thrones, two curtains were pulled back and out walked Beira followed by a male and the female I'd seen earlier with the ornate headdress. They walked together, hand in hand, and moved to sit in the chairs with Beira standing just to the right of them. Who were they that the Great Mother was not seated yet they were?

"Thank you all for joining us this night," the male spoke in a deep voice. "I'd like you all to welcome our guests, Novaleigh and Gavin." He raised his hand and pointed to us, and the crowd turned in our direction.

I lifted my hand and gave a faint wave. I didn't know what to say or what to do. Gavin seemed a bit more comfortable, but I assumed that was because he'd already mingled with them before I arrived. Beira inclined her head in our direction, and I responded in kind.

"Please, make yourselves at home, my people welcome you with open arms."

"Thank you," I said over the din of the crowd.

As soon as I spoke, the fae offered greetings and went back to what they were doing.

"Follow me," Oliver said as he came up behind us.

"Oliver, where have you been?"

"Never mind that. Let's eat."

"Hey wait," I said as I reached down and touched his shoulder. "Why is the Great Mother not sitting and who are the two people that are?"

"The village had no idea she was coming and weren't prepared. She told them not to fuss, she'll find a seat somewhere, and that is her son and his wife. They are the king and queen of this land," he replied before moving towards the head of the room.

"Oh," I stammered.

"Follow me. We're sitting near the front," Oliver said as he made his way through the crowd.

Gavin and I followed until we reached a long rectangular table set a few feet away from where the king and queen were seated. I stared at them both until we eventually made eye contact. I couldn't help myself. Their beauty was intoxicating, just like all the other fae I've met here in Sacrife, and yet there was something different about them…something otherworldly. I didn't want to take my eyes off of them. I inclined my head and mouthed *thank you* to them both before finally looking away.

"Novi, sit here," Oliver said with a smile.

To one side of me was Gavin, and then across the table was Oliver and a female otter. She was smaller than him and her coloring was more fawn than taupe. I could tell though, by the way they interacted, they were connected somehow. She was dressed in a pale green dress with an intricate leaf design cut into the layers of her skirt. She handed him a plate and kissed the tip of his ear before she left to go back to the banquet table. Oliver blushed, and I stared right at him until he was forced to look at me.

"What?" Oliver asked.

"Who was that, Oliver?" I teased.

He was shoveling in food when he stopped mid bite. "Cianna is my mate."

My brow lifted as I stared him down. "Why didn't you tell me you were married?"

"We're not like humans, Novi. Marriage is not really a thing for us. Otters simply mate for life."

I smacked the paw he had lying on the table. "You should've told me you had someone waiting for you. I cannot believe you have been out there with me risking your life and she's been here—worried I can assume."

Gavin chuckled at how Oliver was squirming in his seat.

Cianna came back to the table and took a seat next to Oliver. She was quiet and peaceful with delicate features, and I marveled at what a kind soul she must have to be married to such a selfless person like Oliver.

"Cianna," Oliver offered. "I'd like you to meet Novaleigh and Gavin. They are the ones I've been helping."

"Oh," she stammered as she set down her fork and reached across the table, her paw extended in greeting. "It's delightful to meet you. Oliver has been telling me wonderful things about you. Are you feeling better?" Cianna said in a lilting tone.

I took her paw and shook it gently. "It's pleasure to meet you. Thank you, too, for letting us borrow him. He's been wonderful and very helpful to Gavin and me." Gavin leaned in and offered his hand to Cianna as well.

After we all exchanged pleasantries, Gavin and I left to go grab some food. When we returned, the king, queen, and Beira were also sitting at the table. Oliver and Cianna had shifted to make room for everyone. My breath hitched again when I looked at the stunning young couple. *What is it with the two of them?*

"Hello," I said as Gavin and I sat in the seats across from everyone. "Thank you for welcoming us here. I promise we won't be any trouble."

"I think the most of it is behind you now. Just a bit more to go, and you'll be on your way back home," Beira said with a smile.

I nodded, unable to speak. *Just a bit more to go. I can do this. I can face what's next.*

Chapter Twenty-One

Beira excused herself shortly after dinner, and the king and queen retired soon thereafter as well. In fact, the entire hall seemed to dissipate, leaving just the four of us. It had been a long day for everyone, and in my heart I knew Gavin and I needed to sleep too, but I had so many questions. Oliver and Cianna offered to stay to answer them for me. I wanted to understand more about this place and why I was here to begin with. Why I was so drawn to the king and queen; why the lands were so different from one another; and how come the fae villages each seemed to be a world unto themselves? Oliver and Cianna obliged all my curiosities and were very helpful in providing the answers I so desperately needed. Oliver said I wasn't ready until now to hear them. I had stopped listening and only judged, but after all I'd endured, that had changed. It was time I knew about Sacrife and why it was so special.

The fae who lived in Hortus were different than the other fae creatures in Sacrife because they were the originals. The king and his betrothed were so intoxicating because it was their nature. Beira's first born son, Dermot, was made in her image and is the one who rules over all the magic within Sacrife. His twin sisters, Una and Uphren are favored in his eyes and granted many blessings. They rule over Aestas and the lands in-between.

His middle sister Lithia, however, was banned to the white and forbidden to ever leave or it would result in her death. Apparently, she tried to kill Dermot's wife, Demile, to take her place and rule at his side. Dark and tragic and very Shakespearean in context, but nonetheless a serious offense punishable by death. Beira apparently pleaded for Lithia's life, not because she deserved it, but because it would upset the balance within Sacrife if she were to die. Beira was the mother of it all and balance had to be maintained, so she vowed to live in The White with Lithia to keep her under control. Dermot agreed, but swore if Lithia ever came close to his family again, he would kill her with his bare hands and not with his magic.

Golar was the youngest of Beira's five children, and while her village is hidden from view, she was no less important to the cycles that fueled the lands. Together they ruled over the seasons within Sacrife. Summer, fall, winter, and spring. Growth, harvest, death, and awakening. Every step I've taken since I arrived here in Sacrife was destined to be, according to Oliver. My fall was the beginning of my growth, my trip to Cadent was about reaping what I had sown, and I needed to die in Hiems in order to wake up here in Hortus. As Beira stated, I have more to learn, but I hope I'm well on my way to finding that place of peace within me. I truly welcome what is to come next or at least I hope I'm up to the challenge.

I hugged Cianna and Oliver and bid them goodnight, thanking them both for helping me—*helping us*, I thought as I reached for Gavin's hand. Without the journey and this crucial moment of understanding, I would still be questioning everything before me. I know now that I must trust what comes next, for there is a plan greater than the one I can see at work. Oliver showed Gavin and me to the home we would live in while we were here, before he and Cianna took off for their burrow. Oliver said he would be gone for a few days but would return when the moon was highest in the sky. I smiled and waved as they left hand in hand.

Gavin and I walked into the stone cottage and were welcomed with a roaring fire and lit candles.

"Oh, this place is beautiful," I said as I turned slowly to take it all in.

"It is," Gavin said as he caught me mid-spin. "It almost reminds me of that place we used to claim as our future home when we were teenagers." My smile dropped. "No, no. That is not why I said it. We're done living in the past, Novi. From this moment forward, we only choose things that move us in that direction, understand?" he said as he kissed me.

"But that place was our dream. We claimed it when we were seventeen and said one day we'd get married and raise a family there."

"And things change, Novi. Now we'll need to find a new dream."

I sighed. "How about we decide to stay here? I like it here. I'm happy for the first time in a long time, Gavin."

He kissed me again and again until the tears that had been rising to the surface dissolved into another emotion. Gavin lifted me and carried me to the bed in the other room. No words were spoken, but I knew exactly what he was telling me by the way he touched me, the way his hands and lips caressed my body. This was my perfect moment. The one I'd choose to be suspended in time in, if that was ever possible—Gavin and I joined together, mind, body, and soul. He was home. He was the peace. Not the "you complete me" cliché but the "no one else makes me feel like myself" kind of completes me.

I've always been the girl who walks into a crowded room and feels alone. I'm social and outgoing, but inside I'm always screaming *'when can I leave'*. Not with him. Gavin makes me want to stay. That's what scared me so much when I was younger. How can that much calm and comfort exist in one person? I still don't know, but I really don't care now. All I want is to have him as my safe place to fall.

Gavin and I spend the rest of the night entangled in one another—lost in our redemption. When the sun began to shine in the windows, I knew it was time to start the day, but I was content in his arms and didn't want to move. A knock at the door changed that. Gavin covered himself with one of the coverings on the bed and answered it on the second knock.

"Good morning, Beira," Gavin said in a lighthearted voice.

"Good morning to you, Gavin. Is the cottage to your liking?" she replied.

"It's great. Much better than our previous accommodations," he teased.

They both were laughing when I walked into the room.

"Good morning, Novi."

I smiled. "You remembered."

She inclined her head with a grin.

"What brings you here?" I asked as Gavin excused himself to put on some clothes.

"You. Are you ready for today?"

"Oh. So we're starting right away?"

She looked at me inquisitively. "Are you not the one who said you were ready to leave?"

"Um, yes," I stammered. "I did."

"Something changed?"

"I'm at peace here in Hortus, and I'm afraid of changing anything to upset that."

She nodded. "Change is inevitable, Novi."

"I know, but I haven't felt like this in a very long time, and I wanted to enjoy it for a minute or two."

Beira stood silent for a moment. "Very well. I can grant you that, but when I return next time, this won't be an option. Agreed?"

I nodded quickly. "Thank you."

"You're welcome." She smiled. "Feel free to roam about. Nothing will harm you or come after you here, Novi. You're safe to just be, but please know, the longer you are here, the more soul searching you may encounter. This part of Sacrife is magical in that way, nothing anyone says or does can change that, it just is."

"Okay."

"If and when you do find something, please face it head on. You've come too far not to," Beira said as she turned to leave. "Embrace the journey."

I smiled back at her. She already knew what I was going to face but didn't want to say, I knew it and could feel it in my soul. I'd take her challenge and see her one beyond it. *You hope.* "No, I know."

"You know what?" Gavin asked as he toweled off his wet hair. "Where is Beira?"

"She left. You and I are free to roam the land. Care to go on a grand adventure?"

"With you," he teased. "Nah."

"Jerk," I laughed as I chased him back into the bedroom.

We fell onto the bed in a tangle of arms and legs that eventually led to an epic pillow fight. I had no idea how or why, the things in this cottage were exactly like they would be in my and Gavin's world, but I assumed it had something to do with Beira and Dermot's magic and their wanting us to feel at home and comfortable here. Problem was, their world was becoming too comfortable. The perfect retreat from the world I so desperately wanted to escape. I was serious when I told Gavin I wanted to stay here. There weren't any demons or shitty choices here, just happiness and freedom. I was free—finally.

Chapter Twenty-Two

We walked through the village and beyond its limits into the forest. The trees were lush and thick with dark and pale green leaves. The trunks were larger than a man could wrap his arms around, and the bark was aged and weathered with knots and layers showing its age and trials. They stood like statues, but the rustle of the leaves soothed the soul as the wind blew across the branches. The sound was perfect—tranquil. There were trees like this near my grandparents' house too. Gavin and I used to go out there on those warm summer days and lie against the roots. There was no other sound like that of being one with the earth. It was like the ancients intended. I thought back to the stories my Pappa used to tell about the old gods and their connection to nature. It was the reason he chose the plot of land he did. It called to him, and he knew that was where he would spend the rest of his days.

I know when they found him that day he'd been out for a walk. I can only hope he was in his favorite spot by the water's edge when the stroke decided to claim him. I did a lot of reading about strokes once he passed. I needed to know why that was the way his body decided to give out. Had Nanna been with him he may have had a chance of some recovery, but then again, living debilitated would've killed him too. Maybe a quick and painless death was a blessing. I know he would've considered the other alternative a curse.

I ran my hands along the tree bark and felt the rough, furrowed edges and said a little prayer to the man who made me believe in something bigger than myself. *Thank you, Pappa for your love and guidance. I'm sorry I disappointed you with my choices as of late, but maybe I'll get the chance to turn that around and make things right here soon. I love you, Pappa. I hope you're in your heaven and taking long lazy naps with the spring air blowing across the cool water and bouncing off the trees. I hope you and Nanna are dancing in the rays of sunlight like you used to when I was a kid. Peace and love to you, Pappa. Peace and love.*

I jumped when the wood beneath my fingers twisted and moved. I ran over to Gavin and we both watched as the bark on the tree shifted into a weathered face and yawned before it spoke.

"I had hoped I would see you while you were on this journey."

My hands shook and my heart began to race. It wasn't possible. Not even remotely. *Have you forgotten where you are, Novi? Everything here does things that aren't possible.* My brain struggled, but my heart settled when he spoke again.

"Star light, star bright, have ye seen my little Novi tonight? I wish I may, I wish I might, have a hug from my sweet girl this night."

"Pappa," I whispered.

I heard Gavin gasp under his breath. "I'll be damned."

"It's good to see you two together again. Your nanna and I always knew ye were destined to be. She saw it in the tea leaves more times than I can count, said ye two were flames or somethin' like that."

I laughed through sniffles and ran back to the tree, wrapping my arms around it as best I could. "I've missed you."

"I've missed ye too, Novi."

"I have so much to ask you and so much I want to say."

"Tut-tut-tut. Nonsense. I won't hear of anything if it involves apologies. There is nothin' here to ask forgiveness for.

I died, Novi. That was the normal course of nature. Ye had nothing to do with that. I died peacefully. At first I thought of ye and your mum, then I briefly thought of your dad…he and I had a lot of unfinished business, but I still thought of how proud I was of him, after all, he gave me ye. My final thoughts, though, were for my Maureen. She was ma whole world. I was sad I'd be leavin' her but knew I'd always be with her in spirit."

Tears rolled down my cheeks faster than I could wipe them.

"Naw cryin'. I want to see that smile of ye's," the face in the tree said as the bark eyebrows furrowed. "Gavin?"

"Yes, sir," he responded quickly, still taken aback by the talking tree. I could feel his hands trembling as he held mine.

"Ye takin' care of me girl?"

Gavin swallowed hard. "I wasn't for a long time, Mr. Darrow, but I do plan to never let that happen again."

The tree's face went from concerned to happy with the twisting of the bark. "Good. That is all I needed to hear. I'll be watching ye too, Nanna and I both. Take care of each other. Love until ye heart bursts from it, Novi. Stop fearing everything, it's part of ye's journey." The face contorted once more. "I must go now. Talk to me in the forest. I will always hear ye there."

"Please don't go."

"A love ye, Novi," he replied just as the tree went back to its natural state. I laid my forehead where he'd just been and whispered back. "I love you too, Pappa."

I sobbed into the tree for a while and Gavin just held me, giving me the moments I needed to come to terms with what just happened. When I finally turned to face him, he gave me a sad smile. "I really don't know what to think of this place, but since it gave you back to me, I'll accept it with all of its quirks." I laughed through my tears and he wiped my eyes. "It's going to be okay. You are going to be okay," he concluded.

I nodded and laid my head on his chest, his arms wrapping around my body in a protective hug. "Can we go home now?" I said into his shirt.

"*Home* home or back to the cottage?"

I looked up at him, his lips tipped in a grin. "The cottage."

Gavin intertwined our fingers and we headed back through the forest and into the clearing where the village gates stood. The gates had changed since we'd left this morning. They were no longer covered in moss and vines, but were now blooming with spectacular roses in all of my favorite colors. I smiled and knew just who had made it possible. *Thank you, Pappa.*

When I was twelve, he built a greenhouse out of old windows and doors. It was his way of bringing my favorite fairytale to life. He gave Nanna a library and me, the roses. My heart swelled thinking of the love he had to give. Today was painful, but it was a blessing too. I was grateful to have had the chance to experience them both.

As we made our way through the gates, Dermot and Demile were waiting to greet us. "How was your walk?"

"Blessed."

Dermot inclined his head with a slight grin. "Hortus has a way of blessing us each and every day. Would you and Gavin care to join us? There is someone to whom we'd like you to meet."

I looked over at Gavin. "We'd be happy to," he replied for both of us.

"This way," Dermot gestured.

Chapter Twenty-Three

It took some time to get to where we were going, and even then I was still lost as to where we were. Dermot and Demile had been gracious in trying to talk to us about this and that, but I could hardly pay attention. I just wanted to know where we were headed and why I kept hearing an annoying tinking sound. They all said they heard nothing and that maybe I was just hearing fairy chimes. *It's not damn fairy chimes. What the hell are fairy chimes anyway?*

"Here we are," Dermot announced.

Demile stopped at the bottom of a stone staircase that was covered in dense green clumps of flowerless plants and grass. It curved slightly on its way upwards until it ended at an enchanted looking cottage.

"Up there?" I pointed.

"Yes," Demile replied.

I took a deep breath and tugged on Gavin's arm.

"Sorry, Novaleigh, but this visit is for you only. Gavin needs to stay here with us."

"But…"

"We will keep him company, not to worry."

I gave Gavin a confused glance, but he nodded in the direction of the cottage. "You've got this. I'll be here waiting."

"It's an empty forest. What are you all going to do?"

Dermot grinned and waved his hand in a circular motion until a portal opened. The watery circle expanded and spread out until a target range appeared. "Care to try your hand at archery?"

"Yeah," Gavin exclaimed as if he were a twelve year old boy.

"Wait! Before you guys go off to play like kids, care to explain what I'm supposed to be doing? You said 'visit'. Who am I supposed to be visiting?"

"The weaver," Demile offered. "She requested your presence. Said it was of great importance.

"The weaver," I repeated as if saying it again was going to clarify who in the hell this person was.

"You needn't fear her. She will guide you to the answers you seek, and when you are finished, you will know which path you are intended to take."

I stared at Demile blankly. I had wanted to go home since I arrived, and now I felt content. The idea that this "weaver" was going to upset my happiness had me feeling anxious. I didn't want to go up those stairs. I didn't want anything to change. *Change sucks!*

"But it is inevitable," a voice behind me spoke.

"Beira?"

She smiled and waved me up. "Stop fearing and start hoping. You may just be surprised by the outcome."

I swallowed hard and took the first step, then the second, and so on. When I reached the top, I looked down at Gavin, Dermot, and Demile who all were giving me encouraging looks. I gave them a quick wave and followed Beira into the cottage.

"This place looks like it belongs in a Grimm fairytale movie. I love all the paned windows."

Beira laughed. "Just through the archway there you will find the weaver. When you are finished, we will all be waiting for you."

I bit my lip and nodded as Beira closed the door. Inside was quaint and looked like the home of someone who prided themselves on preserving nature. There were bundles of herbs hanging from the rafters in the ceiling, along with flowering plants set on round tables. There was also a built-in bookshelf against the far wall with all sorts of knickknacks. Crystals in varying shapes and sizes, glass bottles labeled and filled with different colored objects. There were also all kinds of old, tattered books lining the shelves above the jars. The smell was a mixture of rosemary and sage, but there were also ones that I couldn't recognize by scent alone. A portly grey cat stretched in the wide sill of the window before it curled into a ball, letting the sun warm it.

"I'm in here," a woman's voice called out.

I followed the sound and found an older woman with ginger and grey hair sitting in a rocking chair, knitting.

"Hello," I said softly.

"Hello, Novaleigh. Have a seat," she said as she pointed to the chair across from her. "My name is Oona. It's a pleasure to see you in person." I gave her a quizzical look. "I've seen you in my dreams." She smiled and continued knitting.

I sat down in the chair, all the while staring at the woman across from me. My mom's name sounded almost the same, and her hair color was similar too, yet something about her was very different. It seemed like I was viewing my mom through a hazy filter. I couldn't stop staring. I thought about everyone while I was here in Sacrife, but I'd yet to think of her—until now. I was so close to her and yet she'd not been my first thought. I wondered why. Too painful, maybe? I didn't know, but it didn't really matter. I was here, in this moment, with a water colored version of her.

"You hadn't thought of your mom because she has been with you all throughout this journey, guiding you—her and your nanna."

"You can hear my thoughts like Beira, huh?"

She winked.

"How do you? Never mind," I quickly added.

"You ever knit?" Oona asked as she leaned over and handed me needles and some yarn. "It's good for the mind and the soul," she added before I even had a chance to respond.

She stood and showed me how to start and make a slip knot and how to *cast on*, as she called it. I was totally confused but after a few more tries, I was knitting a tiny bit. Oona continued on with her lesson until I had made a row. "There you go, see now, you're knitting. You're a natural it seems," Oona said as she sat back down and resumed her own project.

"What am I making?"

"I think we should start off small with a tea cozy, and then we can move on to bigger and better things."

I nodded and went back to my stitches. I'm not sure how long we sat there in silence, but it seemed like forever. I wanted to ask why I was here, but I didn't want to be the first to speak. And though she could hear my thoughts, she gave me nothing that would help answer my confusion. We continued on in silence.

"Why did you go to the bridge that day, Novaleigh?" Oona finally spoke.

My needles made a clink. *Hey, was that the sound I'd heard walking here? No, focus, Novi. Lie or tell the truth? Truth always. Shit, she can read my thoughts, of course—the truth, or she'll know you're lying.*

"I went for a walk, and then I thought I saw something in the water and walked closer to the edge to see. That's all."

"Is it?"

"Yes. I saw an otter once and thought I saw two in the water so I looked. I had no idea that there was loose rock beneath my feet. I slipped a bit, but I caught myself."

"Did you really?"

My shoulders dropped. "What are you implying?"

"I'm not implying anything. I just want to make sure you are being completely honest with yourself. Had you not been thinking about how bad the world felt to you with everything that transpired over the past few months?"

"Yes, but not to the degree you're implying."

"So you really don't know what happened to you that day?"

"That is what happened. I was on the bridge near my grandparent's house and thought I saw two otters playing in the water, I went to look, slipped and somehow landed here in Sacrife. Being here is the only confusing part. I have no idea how I ended up in a magical land filled with fae and monsters." I blurted, my frustration reaching a boiling point. "I'm sorry. I'm not trying to be rude, but all of this," I waved my hands around, "and you and this place. It's craziness."

"I agree, but it's all your creation, Novaleigh. Your design."

"What are you talking about?"

"I'm a weaver. I'm what is connecting this world to the world you come from. My purpose is to show you your choices."

I sat in silence as she continued on.

"You came here on your own accord. That day, you did slip and fall, but that is not all that happened. You hurt yourself and Sacrife has been your escape, but now you have a choice to make, stay here or choose to return to life. Here you're only existing. Once they turn the machines off, it will be up to you where you want to be."

My mind went wild. Suddenly, I was thrust into two realities. The air around me was cool and dry. It was dusk when I went out for a walk, and I felt a little shaky after the wine—*after seeing Gavin.* The moon had yet to show itself and the sunset was my favorite shades of pink, purple, and blue. I wanted to see the water. I'd hoped it would soothe me the way it used to. My mind shifted to Gavin and me and us going out on the weekends to see if we could spot the otters. Usually we saw them by the house we'd hoped to live in someday. Then, I met Winston and Oliver here in Sacrife. The tinking sound was there again in the distance. I fell. The water was so cold. I saw the blood and felt as though I was drowning. My head hurt. My body ached everywhere, and my vision was blurry. What happened? Where was I?

"She needs an MRI. Get all the blood work I requested, and call her next of kin."

"Yes, doctor."

People were scurrying about, and I was so cold. Someone put a blanket on me, and I wanted to thank them, but I couldn't speak. Maybe I'd spoken and they didn't hear me because they were so busy. I was in a tunnel. A loud thumping tunnel with music playing in the background. I could hear voices but couldn't make out what they were saying. It was broken and sing-songy like the twin queens. They're here. My hair was pink. No, not pink. Stained with blood and tinted that hue. Where was I?

"I'm here, Novi. Oh my god, what happened to you?"

Mom?

A firm but quiet voice spoke. "I'm afraid your daughter is in a coma."

"What?" my mother cried.

"She suffered severe head trauma when she fell on the rocks. No one knows how long she was there before she was found so we cannot say for certain the extent of the damage at this time. We have her on a ventilator for now because she intermittently stops breathing. Until we can assess her situation more, she will remain like this."

I heard my mother sobbing before she asked.

"Who found her?"

"I'm not sure, but if he hadn't she would've died."

Died? Oh my God.

"Do you have any idea how long she'll be like this?"

"The first 24 hours are the most crucial. We'll just have to wait and see."

"I'm in a coma? That is where I've been, not here in Sacrife? Why...then how...I don't understand," I questioned Oona.

"You are in the in-between. You called it lost and happy, except those weren't accurate descriptions. Your choices are death or life."

"Death or life, what does that mean?"

"It means that this is the final piece of the puzzle, Novaleigh, and you have to decide whether you are going to stay here in Sacrife or go back to your life and live until you are old and grey."

"So here in Sacrife is death? It doesn't feel like death. Not now at least. I mean it did at first but then it didn't. It felt right and comfortable. I'm here with Gavin," I babbled.

Oona looked up from her knitting. "Sacrife is sacrifice...the land of the lost. At some point all the things you are experiencing will fade away just as you will. Life is one continuous flow and someday you'll return to live again. You'll live many lifetimes, Novaleigh, and you'll need to learn and grow in each one. However, you must know that in the next lifetime you may not know anyone like your mother or your Nanna and Pappa. You may not even know Gavin in the same way. You two are twin flames so it's likely you'll encounter one another at some point, but you may not be lovers in the next life. You could just be friends. Nothing is guaranteed with free will."

"Oh."

"Why not live now? You have what you want right in front of you. Go home. Embrace love and all it has to offer."

"But I don't have Gavin there? Or Pappa? All of that forgiveness and understanding is here."

"Don't be so sure. Things may be different than you think," Oona said before going back to her knit one, purl one.

"Gavin, its Euna." I could hear the distress in my mom's voice. *"Did you by chance happen to have been the one to find Novi? Oh no, I thought you were the one. No, she's not okay. She's in a coma. Yes, I'm here at the Portree. Okay. See you then."* My mom cried as she hung up the phone. She reached for my hand and rubbed it with her thumb. *"I'm here, Novi. Listen to my voice and come back to me. Please. I need you. I can't lose you, too."*

Tears streamed down my face. "Why are you making me live this?"

"Because you need to see that you are loved, and you will be missed if your choice is to stay here," Oona said with a sad smile.

"Any change in her status?"

"No, Gavin. No change."

"I got here as soon as I could. Are you okay?" Gavin asked.

"As good as can be expected."

Gavin sat on the other side of the bed and reached for my hand. I laid there unconscious, my mom on one side and the man I loved on the other, and I had no way to let them know I was here, listening. I wanted to scream "I'm here. I'm right here."

"They can't hear you."

"I know, but I can wish for it."

"Yes, you can. Wish away, but let me ask you, where has that gotten you?"

I felt like I was just slapped. What had my wishes produced other than heartache? I had big dreams, but when I got to the place to finally make them come true, I chickened out. I convinced myself it was too hard, too big of a dream, and I settled for being someone's assistant. Sure, we all need to learn and grow, but when we squelch our intuition and let someone else berate our dreams, a piece of us dies. We begin to think we're not worthy of more because we listen to the lies.

"You don't know what you're talking about. I've been doing this job for thirty years and you've been at it for five minutes. I decide the talent. You need to learn from my experience." True but only to an extent. Age and wisdom does not always equal wiser. Sometimes the old can gain more knowledge from listening to the new. It should be symbiotic. When did learning become a straight line?

When we are down on our own self-image, something else happens to challenge us. Another hitch or two and we die a little more. At least we think we do because we've let our demons consume us. Our inner dialogue suddenly becomes truth, and we are left empty and alone. Fear of failure has robbed us of our once amazing dreams. Nanna and Pappa always told me I could have it all within reason, but then I saw my parents fail at having a marriage and a life, and so I believed that would be the same case for me. I couldn't have my dream of writing and publishing and have Gavin too. It was too big of a dream. I gave up half of myself to dump it into the other. Now, here I am, dying for all intents and purposes and have effectively lost it all. How was I going to get back to a place where I could make positive choices when all I've done is fail?

"Have you really failed? I've seen a lot of accomplishment mixed with trial and error."

"Gah. I keep forgetting that you're here in my head with me. No thought is sacred."

She gave me a smug grin. "It's the weaver in me. I cannot help myself."

"Why are you called the weaver, you're knitting?" I quipped.

"I do more than knit, but that is not why I'm called the weaver, Novaleigh." Oona put down her needles and looked at me. "There are threads that exist through time. Like fate lines, in a way, but these lines aren't just for one lifetime. They are the threads for all your life journeys." I shook my head in confusion. "Unlike a seer, I can see all of your threads. My job is to help weave the timelines together. I try and keep you on your true path."

"But you said something about free will, earlier. How does that affect a person's threads?"

"Let me put it another way to help you understand. Have you ever been on a boat?"

"Once."

"Okay then, imagine you are the captain of this boat. You control the boat and its course, but sometimes you encounter a storm, and you become disoriented and lose sight of the shore. You try and get back on track, but you're lost and you need guidance to get back to where you were going. Weavers try and get you back on course. Problem is, things have changed in you from your experience. You're more cautious, you fear things on the path to your destination, and you make rash decisions—free will. You can do one of two things; give up and turn back, or you can decide to press forward into the unknown. However, now you're afraid of what's ahead. You lack faith. That is where I come in. I'm here to show you the way. I weave the past, the present, and the future so the threads become visible, and you begin to see the light. Does that make sense?"

"I think so."

"Novaleigh, it's simple. Nothing is as bad as it seems at the time, and sometimes in the midst of the hell you're enduring is your pivot point, the place where you can get back your focus and turn your life around. Stop thinking about all that is wrong, and focus on what is right. It's there that you'll step out of the crazy, rise out of the rabbit hole, and start living again."

I had nothing to say in response to all that. She was right, but I wasn't ready to admit that just yet. Once I stopped bugging her with questions, Oona went back to her knitting. I don't think she was annoyed or anything, but simply wanted me to make my own choice. Something I was apparently incapable of doing at this time. I knew it in my heart what I should do, but there was a part of me that was still undecided. I looked over at the almost completed blanket lying at the edge of Oona's worn shoes and realized how long we'd been together here in this house. Then again, she was the expert. Her fingers were flying as the needles worked their magic in her gifted hands. I, however, still fumbled along barely crafting half a coaster. I didn't put too much stock in my failed project though, because my mind was elsewhere. I kept drifting between this world and the one where I was comatose.

"Euna, you really should get some rest. Go back to the house and take some time for yourself. I'll stay with her and let you know if anything changes."

"You're a good man, Gavin Kirkpatrick," my mother replied with a soft smile. "You'll let me know right away if anything changes, yes?"

"In an instant."

She nodded and put on her coat before leaning down. "I love you, Novi. Come home." A moment later she was walking out the door and it was just Gavin and I—alone.

"Novi, please." Gavin pleaded as he kissed my hand. "You don't have to be with me or here in Scotland. No one is putting any boundaries on you, but you have to come back to us. I'd settle for just knowing you were alive and well at this point."

He laid his head on my hand, and I felt the warmth of his skin and the moisture of his tears. Maybe he did still care. Maybe if I sat up right now and said I'm sorry, he'd forgive me. *Yeah, out of pity.*

"Give me the chance to explain myself to you, Novi. One more chance."

What does he need to explain? I'm the asshole here.

"I miss you, Novi."

He misses me? Like here in Sacrife…no, my mind…no, here in the in-between.

I looked up at Oona. "All right." I declared. "I find my faith, get back my focus, and then what? How am I supposed to get from here to there?"

Oona reached over and placed her hand on mine. "First you have to forgive yourself and then you have to fall."

I scoffed. "You're kidding right?"

She shook her head, picked up her needles, and went right back to knitting.

The tinking sound echoed again, and I looked around wondering where it was coming from. "What is that? Why do I keep hearing that?"

"That is the ventilator. The doctors want to take you off of it to see if you'll breathe on your own. It's then you'll have to decide, Novaleigh. Sacrife or home."

"When?"

"Soon. You've been on it for forty-eight hours, but in the past six you've shown improvements. They're hoping you'll be well enough to be taken off."

"I see." I sighed. "Is that something I am going to do here with you?"

"No. Our time is through. Now it's time for you to go back to the village with Gavin, Dermot, Demile, and Beira. They have something planned for you."

Chapter Twenty-Four

The five of us were back to the village in a matter of seconds, once I left Oona's cottage. Dermot opened a portal, jetting us back to their home in an instant. When we arrived, there was a full-on celebration—food, music, dancing, the whole nine yards.

"What's going on? I thought I had to do a few things and make some choices so I could move on."

"You do," Beira replied. "We thought you'd enjoy the opportunity to say goodbye here first."

"Yeah, you can't go back without saying goodbye," Oliver teased.

"You're back!" I exclaimed as I bent down to hug him. "Did you know all this? The truth of me the whole time?"

He nodded.

"I'm your guide. Oona thought it best if you had something comforting, a figure that brought you peace and happiness to follow you through the changes. You always did like otters." He grinned.

"I love otters," I said with a kiss on his cheek.

"I'm going to go grab something to eat, I'll find you in a bit," Oliver said before he bid Beira a good afternoon.

"Care to go for a walk with me?"

"Sounds nice."

"You look well. Did you have a good visit with Oona?" Beira asked as we moved away from the crowd.

"I did. It was certainly eye opening to realize all this is just in my mind." I tossed my hands in the air. "Like right now. I'm talking to myself essentially."

"Actually you're not. The weaver and I are real. She in her true form and I in a divine one."

"I'm so confused. Real. Not real. Alive and yet not alive. You do understand why I can't wrap my brain around this, right?"

"You are real, you are alive. Those are facts."

"So then tell me this, Beira, what have I yet to come to terms with? I want to be ready to return when the doctors finally get around to pulling the plug."

"Straight to the truth then?"

"Seems ridiculous not too."

"What is the one thing you've chosen not to come to terms with since you've been here?"

I shook my head and flipped my hands. "I don't know. I've dealt with it all. I made amends to Gavin and I even was able to say my piece to Pappa. There is nothing else."

"Truth, Novi. You can't leave without full honesty."

"What, myself? Am I supposed to say 'I'm sorry, self, for all my shitty choices?'" I replied sarcastically and then quickly realized I'd cursed. "Sorry for the language."

Beira gave a dismissive wave as she sat down on a bench. "Sit."

I reluctantly sat. This was dragging out. I could only hear the tinking sound intermittently now, and I worried the longer Beira and I took to get to whatever it was I needed to accept, that I would lose my window and my chance to go home.

"No disrespect intended, but can you spell it out for me. Assume I'm an idiot, please."

Beira reached for my hand. "You've put it away so carefully that you don't even acknowledge it. I understand why, but that is what we need to tap into, Novi."

The realization of what she was referencing rose to the surface. *Nanna.* I never dealt with Nanna. Too much guilt and shame. She was my world—my everything, and when she needed me the most, I dismissed her. My problems were bigger than hers. She couldn't understand what I was going through, no one could. Sure, people would listen and offer advice, but what good was that. It wasn't a solution. The tears and the pain slammed into me with enough force to bring me to my knees. I sat there, grass and leaves scratching at my flesh as I cried.

"That's it, Novi. Let it all go. None of what happened was your fault."

"Wasn't it?" I sobbed.

Beira knelt down next to me. "No, it wasn't. Your Pappa passed away, a normal course of action in life, even he told you that."

I nodded.

"Maureen didn't blame you, Novi. In fact, it was quite the opposite. She knew where your head was at, and she knew you needed to find your path on your own terms, in your own time."

"How do you know that?"

"I know," Beira said as I watched her change. Her long auburn hair transformed into a shorter grey with soft curls framing her face.

My body shook and my chest constricted. "Nanna?"

She pushed back my hair. "It's me, sweet girl."

I wrapped my arms around her neck and cried. "I'm sorry. I'm so, so sorry."

"Novi, please stop apologizing."

"I can't. When you called me that day and I said I had to call you back, that I was in the middle of something, I wasn't doing anything I couldn't have put on hold. I had no idea those would be the last words I'd ever get to speak to you. You died, and I didn't get to tell you I loved you or how much you meant to me or that I was sorry. I didn't make you a priority."

She brushed my hair back again, just like she used to when I was a little girl lying in her lap. "I already knew those things. Nothing you could say or not say would change how much I love you. You were a gift to me the moment I laid eyes on you."

"But…"

"No, I won't accept any more of the lies you tell yourself. None of them are true."

I nodded and leaned into her embrace. I don't know how long we stayed like that, but for me it didn't matter. The tinking sound didn't matter. I was here with my nanna again. Safe and happy.

"Novi?"

I looked up at her smiling face. "Tell me everything that's been going on. What is happening with you and Gavin?"

"Really?"

She nodded and we started talking. It was just like old times when I'd tell her about all that was going on, and she'd laugh and offer advice when needed. We were together. My eyes drifted closed as Nanna held me in her arms.

"Novi, it's time for me to go now."

"No," I said sleepily.

"Promise me something."

"Yes, ma'am."

"Go back to your mom and Gavin. They need you just as much as you need them."

"But I'm happy here."

"This happiness is only a façade. If you want true happiness...go home."

"We're just waiting on her most recent blood work to come in, and we'll move on to the next phase."

"Thank you, doctor." I heard my mother say.

"She's been restless. Is that a good sign?" Gavin questioned.

"I'm hoping, but I cannot say for certain. There has been an increase in her brain activity, so we'll see. I'll be back later this afternoon."

When I opened my eyes, Beira and I were sitting on the bench, talking as if none of that happened.

"Novi, it's time we head back. It's almost time for me to leave, and I've taken you away from your party long enough."

I shut my eyes and rubbed my forehead. *I'm losing it again.* What is real and what is clutter in this fractured mind? I could no longer tell. Beira stood and I followed. We were back amongst the villagers and Gavin was asking me to dance.

"Where have you been?"

I shook my head. "I don't know."

He kissed me, and we joined the frivolities. Oliver and Cianna were there, while Dermot and Demile sat in high backed seats made of a variety of spring flowers.

Everything was blissful.

Everything was a blur.

Chapter Twenty-Five

Dusk was settling in, and the party was winding down. The sky was once again the stunning hues of blue, pink, purple.

"Is it like this every night in Hortus, Oliver?"

"Yes. It's perfect isn't it?"

"It is."

Beira passed by as she walked with Dermot and Demile towards the tree line. I wondered why she didn't say anything, but I didn't try and stop her either, for fear she'd want to hash out my issues once more. I'd made my choice, now I just needed to follow through with it.

"Excuse me," Oliver said in a rush before running over to Beira's side.

She leaned down, and he nodded his head before looking back at me. *Oh great. She's done with me, but now he's going to be after me to make my peace.*

A moment later Oliver was back by my side, and I couldn't help myself, I had to ask. "What did she say?"

"That you were ready, and I was to make the preparations immediately. Are you ready to go?"

"That's it? No 'Goodbye, you've been through the ringer and then some?' Just an, 'I'm all done and I'm out?'" Oliver looked at me curiously. "Sorry. Slang term for I'm leaving and have nothing more to say."

"That's not true. She had a lot to say but felt it best for you to stay in your moment without any further distractions."

"Oh," I said half-aloud.

I turned to look over at Beira as she was saying goodbye to her Dermot and Demile and smiled when she waved.

"I wasn't leaving you. I'm trusting you and the person you've become. I'm always with you, Novi. Find me when you can. I'll be waiting. Until then, my sweet girl."

"Wait, what? Where are you going?"

"Home. Just like you, Novi."

Dermot and Demile moved and Beira closed her eyes. In the next moment I was mesmerized. The bottom of Beira's dress was fanning out and taking root in the ground where she stood. The dark green fabric was morphing into grey-green bark and shifting from flowing to solid. Her long red hair was fanning out as the wind whipped around her in a whirlwind of leaves and twigs. Beira's body was changing from human to—a tree? *This is it. The final straw. I'm not in a coma. No, I'm mentally ill with no hope of recovery. She's real in the divine form, but oh no, she's a tree. Novaleigh, fall, die, breathe, at this point just do anything to make this madness end. Enough is enough.*

I looked down at Oliver. "You don't seem surprised by this."

He shook his head. "I'm not. None of us are. She does it all the time."

"Sure. All the time. People turning into trees is completely normal. I'll bite. Why does she turn into a tree all the time, Oliver?" I snapped.

Oliver stepped back, and Gavin came up behind me. "What's wrong, Novi?" Gavin questioned.

My body trembled as I stared at the tree that was Beira. "That." I pointed. "Beira is now a tree and it seems it happens all the time. I wanted to know why." My voice a bit louder than I intended.

"Okay, reasonable question, but that doesn't explain why you are so upset."

"She's gone. Just like that, gone, and soon I will be too. I'm all alone."

Gavin intertwined our fingers. "Not alone. Not anymore."

"And she's not gone, Novaleigh." Oliver offered. "She has to return to the white to watch over Lithia, and this is her way of leaving something for us to remember her by until we see her again. Nothing more. She's with us always this way. In the air, the trees, the leaves, all of it," he said with a soft smile.

I nodded and swallowed hard. My hands were still shaking, and I was suddenly very cold. Shivers ran up my spine, and I couldn't stop from trembling.

"Novi, what's wrong?" Gavin said as he rubbed my hands to warm them.

The tinking sound had fallen silent. The voices in the distance chattered, and the space that was once filled with muffled sounds had now fallen silent.

I looked down at Oliver. "I want to go home now."

He gave a quick nod and rushed to Dermot and Demile who understood, too, the sense of urgency that was beckoning me.

Dermot took a drop of water from a leaf and let it roll over his fingertips for a moment. It began to grow until it was the width of his wingspan. He flicked his hands, twisting the water portal from flat horizontal to vertical. "Let's go," he said as he pointed to the now open space in the water portal.

Demile stepped through first with Dermot's help, then Cianna and Oliver, followed by myself and Gavin. At first, everything was pitch black, and I felt disoriented. When I let my eyes adjust though, I realized where I was—where this all began. The expansive lake where I arrived. The place I splashed water accidentally on Winston, and where I met the twin queens and Oliver. I looked over at Dermot.

"Here?"

"The place where you first arrived in Sacrife is the same place you will need to return."

"How is she supposed to do that?" Gavin asked.

"Hello."

"Hello."

I turned to see the twin queens side by side, their heads slightly tilted and smiling.

I curtsied in their direction. "It is good to see you again."

"You"

"As"

"Well."

"Brother," Una said in her lilting voice as she inclined her head to him.

"Demile," Uphren said as they hugged.

Oliver bowed. "A pleasure, my queens."

"Always"

"Oliver."

The two queens made their way over to where Gavin and I stood.

"You are different."

"Mother has changed you."

They each said as they played with the ends of my hair.

"This, too, suits you."

I nodded. "I agree, but I do miss the way I looked when I arrived."

"So change."

"You have the strength within you now."

I looked over at Gavin. "Don't look at me," he said, grinning wide. "I will love you no matter what you look like." He reached for my hand.

I closed my eyes and thought of what it was that I wanted. Did I want to keep my black hair, return to the pink, or go back to blonde? The one thing I knew for certain was that I didn't want the Neapolitan look. I smiled at the thought. I imagined my hair golden and glinting, saw myself as I once was and realized I was not that girl anymore. I was someone new. I needed a different look to suit the new me. Somewhere in-between. I settled on a rich dark brown, hoping it looked as good as I'd imagined in my mind. When I opened my eyes everyone was staring at me. What happened next was beyond my understanding. They all bowed to me. Not a word was spoken, just a reverence I didn't deserve.

I sighed and listened. No tinking sound. I was running out of time. I turned to Dermot. "What do I need to do to get home? My time is limited," I said with a sad smile.

"You have to go out, and then you have to fall down," he replied as he pointed to the cliff in the distance that dropped at least fifty feet into a pool of water emblazoned with fire.

My eyes went wide. "You've got to be kidding."

Dermot shook his head. "I'm afraid not, Novaleigh. It's the final test of your commitment to change."

I ran my hands through my hair. "Trial by fire, huh?"

"Not exactly."

I turned to look at Gavin. I could just stay here and we'd be together, even if it would only last awhile. Something was better than nothing. I stepped closer to him and wrapped my arms around him. "I love you," I whispered.

Gavin gently caressed my cheek. "I'm so grateful for the chance to love you again."

"I have to go now, but I will find you soon. I promise," I replied as I kissed him. "I wish I could take you with me, but I can't. I have to do this alone."

He kissed me again. "I know."

I reluctantly stepped away from him, releasing our hands and walking over to Una and Uphren. "Thank you for everything. Your favor kept me safe and guided me back to a place of peace."

I wasn't sure if it was allowed, but I did it anyway—I hugged them both. They were taken aback at first but returned the hug in kind. "You're welcome," they said in unison.

Only a few more thank you's to go, and I was ready to accept my fate. I had no idea if falling was going to work, but it was my only option at this point. I didn't attempt to hug Dermot and Demile. They radiated an energy I was afraid to touch, power so big it felt electric. Instead, I bid them farewell with all of my gratitude. I asked them to take care of Oliver and Cianna, Beira, and Gavin for as long as he would be here. I didn't know what would happen to him without me being a part of Sacrife, but I felt like if he were here on his own accord, he deserved their favor. They agreed and wished me well but also urged my departure.

"I can send you close with Oliver as your guide, Novaleigh, but you must not delay any longer," Dermot stated matter-of-factly.

"I understand."

He opened another water portal and sent Oliver and I to the place where I needed to fall. When the portal closed I dropped to my knees. Fear gripping me. "How am I supposed to just fall off a cliff, Oliver?"

He lifted my chin to meet his eyes. "Faith." Tears filled my eyes. "Look at all you've endured since you've been here. Did you think you would've survived that?"

I shook my head.

"But you did. You will survive this too," he said as he wiped a tear from my cheek. "And just think, the real Gavin is just a thought away. He's waiting for you. He and your mom."

"I know," I cried. "I'm going to miss you, Oliver."

"I will miss you too, Novi, but we'll see each other again one day. I'm sure of it."

I bit my lip as my chin trembled. I hugged Oliver tightly and finally released him when I found the strength to move. "Okay. Let's do this."

Oliver guided me to the edge. The waves crashed against the rocks down below and the pink and blue flames danced over the surface. I had no idea if they were real or not, and at this point, I didn't really care. It was time to go home. Time to live a new life.

"Will the flames burn? Will I drown in the crashing waves?"

"Just breathe, Novi."

I looked down one last time and realized I didn't want to fall head first. I thought about how Gavin and I used to make a game of falling with our arms spread wide into the fairy pools and thought that was how I wanted all this to end—Gavin and I falling backwards into the unknown, all the while praying for the outcome we dreamed of.

"Goodbye, Oliver," I said as I stepped backwards and fell off the cliff.

Chapter Twenty-Six

I fell into the water with a large splash and sunk like a stone. My feet guided the way as I drifted further into the murky depths.

Down.

Down.

Down.

The water around me was freezing and felt as if my bones were going to snap from the pressure. It was the same way I felt when I arrived. The only difference was, this time I wasn't afraid.

"Breathe," Oliver's voice reminded me.

I coughed and sputtered as I took my first breath. When I opened my eyes, my mom and Gavin were at my side, crying out their thank you's and gratitude to an unseen force. I was out of the coma. I was back…I was home. I focused my eyes on my mom and squeezed her hand as I looked at her beautiful face. Then I turned to Gavin. The love in his eyes was unmistakable, and I knew we'd weathered yet another storm.

He looked almost the same as the Gavin in Sacrife, the only difference was the scruff around his face. I went to speak, but my voice was only a whisper. "Hi."

His eyes filled with tears. I'd only ever seen him cry once before and that was after his mother died, but these tears were different. There was no sadness, only joy.

Gavin squeezed my hand harder and kissed my fingertips. "Welcome home."

One Year Later...

It's been a year since I fell and woke up. I'm much better now and about a thousand times happier. I started this journal as a way of documenting my thoughts. I don't ever intend on sharing it with the world, but who knows, maybe there's a story in here somewhere. It certainly has all the elements of a great fairytale.

Today is exactly one year to the day since I was in Sacrife with the fae and Oliver. It seems like only yesterday and what a difference a year can make. The doctors told me I had an out of body experience because I was so close to death, but I know in my heart it really happened. I was in the land of the Fae and met some truly amazing beings.

When I was well enough, I flew home to New York and said goodbye to the city that never slept. Not because I didn't love it, but because Scotland and a new life were waiting for me, and it was time to go. I sold my furniture, shipped everything that was sentimental and of value back home, and said goodbye to everyone who mattered to me here, including Mr. Kline and Ethan. I didn't do it for them, I did it for me. I wanted to start the new chapter of my life without any baggage. I'd been given a second chance to live the life I'd dreamt about, and I wasn't going to let anything stand in my way.

I learned a lot in Sacrife. I learned how to live with my demons instead of letting them control me. I still have my bad days, but don't we all? It's a part of living. The sacrifice you have to make to feel the good. If you never experienced loss or pain, how would you know what it felt like to embrace happiness in its purest form? I don't ask those questions anymore. Instead, I exist in a place of gratitude whenever fear and doubt creep in.

Not much still exists of my former life other than my love of reading and editing. I live in my grandparent's house. I work from home, reading manuscripts for publishers and giving them my thoughts, and I don't take on more than I can handle, but I read every day. I also write now. Originally, I thought I'd write about my journey but realized no one would ever believe a story about a girl who lost it all but gained so much more when she fell into a land of magic. So I decided I'd become a children's author and write fairytales. There, I can tell any story I want, no matter how fantastical and people will take away whatever they needed from it. I'm about ninety percent into my first book. Only two people have heard it so far, but they seem to love it. I'll pray the world will too.

I take daily walks out into the forest to visit my trees. Nanna and Pappa are forever with me, Oliver too. There's a family of otters that live just off one of the banks on the property. I know it's not my Oliver, but I imagine it is. It's my greatest joy to envision Oliver and Cianna staying close to watch over me just in case I ever fall again.

My mom still works in Glasgow but spends some weekends and all of her vacations here with us. Gavin and I got married about two and half months after my accident. I didn't see the point in waiting any longer to start the life I should've been living all along. He's doing well. He owns a local pub and manages a restaurant with a buddy of his from London. We have a happy life, and it's about to get even better. We're pregnant. Little Miss is due to arrive any day now. In fact, she's already three days late. I threaten eviction daily but she doesn't listen. Gavin says she's already like me, wanting to do things on her own time and not when she is supposed to. I hope that won't continue to be a theme once she arrives, but I'm certain it's a sign of things to come. God help us all if I ended up with a mini me. I'm hoping she takes after her father.

We've decided to name her Faeth. We thought it suited her and us. I chose to spell it differently to honor those who made her possible, and we both know it took real faith to bring me home. She's our greatest blessing, after the gift of us reuniting. I didn't expect this much happiness, I really didn't. I think when you allow yourself to think about nothing but the things that are going wrong, there's no room to see all that is going right.

Before I fell, I always felt like I was drowning even when I was nowhere near water. Lost in the sea of life with no place to turn. Sure, there were days when I felt as though I could've taken on the world, but on those other days, it was as if my inner dialogue of "I'm not good enough" was threatening to drown me in its dark abyss. The day I let all that fear and worry consume me was the day it all changed. I slipped off that bridge and fell into the void I'd always dreamt about. The thing was, that was also that day I started to live. Odd, but absolutely true. The simplest answer I've been able to come up with for this is—you need to fall before you can rise.

Sacrife taught me that living in the space between life and death was not really living. I thought it was a place where I would feel alive, because in that moment, I just wanted to feel something—anything. Instead, I felt nothing. I think we all have pendulum swings between great happiness and total emptiness, but the key is to lessen the distance between the two emotions. Before my fall, I felt like I was on a ride at the fair where the carnival worker found great humor in letting me suffer because he controlled the lever to make it all stop. But now, I'm in control. Don't get me wrong, I still hate the pendulum swing of emotions because I'm a "I have it all together" kind of gal, but I'm so grateful that I no longer have to deal with it alone. I can be the dichotomy of two beings living within the same body. The difference now is we communicate with one another to embrace the light and the dark. Trust me, grey is a much easier hue to manage.

I often think about my time in Sacrife. The twin queens, Golar, Mabellio, Dermot, Demile, even Lithia and the warden; they all showed me different aspects of myself. Oliver guided me gently, while Beira and Oona, took a more direct approach. I guess it just goes to show that your mind knows all along how to get you to your destiny, but curiosity and free will can sometimes steer you off course. You think you know what's best for you, but you still go a different way. The positive in those experiences is that sometimes you learn your greatest lessons there.

I can only hope that Faeth will learn from my mistakes and make better choices, but my mother says I didn't listen to her advice, so I shouldn't get my hopes up. I had to forge my own path with my own hills and valleys. But I'm certain Faeth will be better than me, because she has Gavin's DNA too, and he's so much better at dealing with things than I am. He's my hero, and I can only assume he'll be hers too.

"Babe, I'm home," Gavin called out from the other room.

"I'm in here. Just writing in my journal."

"You ready to go for our walk?"

I smiled over my shoulder. I never got tired of looking at him. He was standing in the doorway, leaning against the frame. There are times I look at him and see the boy he once was and not the man before me. The thing is, though, his heart and his charm have never changed. He's quirky and odd. He's funny and he makes me feel like a human being—flaws and all. I love him. I've always loved him even when I didn't know it. Gavin is the solid foundation to which we are now building our life upon. Just like Nanna said, he's my querencia.

I told him and my mother every single thing that happened while I was in Sacrife. They believed me—said there was no way I could've made all of that up, it was too personal. Part of me thinks they did it to appease me, but then my mom reminded me of the gift Nanna and I share—clairaudience. She told me my father called it crap, said it was just a ploy of his mother's to get into his head and try and change him, but we knew better. It's funny how I never saw my dad on my journey. It certainly wasn't because I didn't love him or that he didn't matter. It was just that we'd said all we needed to say to one another. There was no unfinished business when it came to he and I—we were, as he liked to call it, square.

I leaned on the desk and pushed up. My back was aching, and I was a bit unstable with my belly protruding two feet in front of me.

"Here, let me help you," Gavin offered.

"I'm really ready for this peanut to come out."

He rubbed my belly. "That is no peanut. It looks like you ate a watermelon."

I slapped his shoulder. "Seriously?"

His smile dropped. "Yes. It seriously looks like you swallowed a watermelon. Maybe two."

I shook my head. "I don't like you."

"Yes you do. You even died and came back from the depths of hell to prove it," he teased as he kissed me. "Come on, walk time."

We made our way out the front door and towards the dirt path leading up to the trees I have now dubbed "Nanna and Pappa". They weren't side by side, but they were in close proximity to one another. Pappa's tree was an old yew tree with a massive trunk and lots of gnarly roots erupting from the ground, and Nanna's tree was an old majestic oak with a glorious canopy. Both, ironically, looked very similar to the trees I encountered in Sacrife. I must've tapped into them and somehow converted the trees I knew so well as a kid to the trees who spoke and provided the guidance I needed. The mind is funny like that, I suppose, pulling this and that from your subconscious to meld them into some form of rational thought. I'm not really sure, but again, I'm grateful I had the chance to say my piece and get the closure I needed, no matter what form it happened in.

"One more little hill and you've got this," Gavin said as he helped me up.

I huffed. "One more feels like I'm climbing a mountain."

When we made it to Nanna's tree, I laid my hand on the trunk. "Hi, Nanna."

Nothing happened, of course, the tree didn't come to life and shift into a human to offer me wisdom and guidance, but just being near it felt like I was close to her. The same happened when I touched Pappa's tree. Just peace and happy memories.

"Do you want to sit and read a bit before we go back inside?"

I shook my head and laughed. "I'm afraid if I sit down, I won't be able to get back up."

"So back to the house then?"

I nodded.

Just then my water broke.

Shock warped my features and Gavin yelled. "What's wrong?"

I bit my lip and said. "She's coming."

"Who?"

I dropped my shoulders and flipped my hands in the air. "Our daughter."

"Oh God," he said as he scrambled to help me.

Gavin and I were making our way back down to the path when I heard voices calling to me. I stopped and turned. *"We're so proud of you, Novi. You and Gavin are going to be great parents. We give our love and blessing to the three of you. Please make sure to bring that beautiful girl to visit us. We can't wait to meet her."* Tears welled in my eyes as the yew and oak shifted into my grandparents, but it wasn't just them. I saw everyone of importance from Sacrife. I smiled and was reminded again, in that moment, Sacrife had been real and we had truly been blessed.

"Honey, are you okay?"

"I am. Can you not see them?" I smiled.

"See who?"

"Them." I pointed.

At first he shook his head and then his face changed. They'd revealed themselves to him, showing him that they were real.

"Well, I'll be damned."

I chuckled. "No, we're blessed." My belly constricted, and I grabbed hold of Gavin's arm and squeezed it tight. "And we are having a baby. I think we need to go."

"Yeah." He looked back and forth between them and me. "Right then."

I took one last look at them and hoped my clairaudience was working. *"See you soon. We love you."*

They waved and watched as Gavin and I made our way to the car. I could still see them in the distance as he drove away from the house. What a blessing. One year to the day—my daughter will be born, and the land of the fae showed itself once more. Miracles do happen as long as we have faith.

When a dream of dying actually becomes a chance to live…all you have to do is fall.

The End

About the Author

Brynn Myers is a paranormal romance author. After considering writing a hobby for years, she finally turned her passion and talent into a career. She came into the paranormal genre later than most but has always loved fairy-tales and all things magical. Using that love, she creates charmed worlds by writing stories involving passionate, strong willed characters with something to discover. Brynn lives with her family in central Florida.

Connect with Brynn in the following places:

Website: http://www.brynnmyers.com
Facebook: https://www.facebook.com/AuthorBrynnMyers
Instagram: https://www.instagram.com/authorbrynnmyers/
Twitter: https://twitter.com/brynnmyers
BookBub: www.bookbub.com/authors/brynn-myers

Brynn Myers

Other Books by Brynn Myers

Jorja Graham
The Life & Death of Jorja Graham (Book 1)
The Echoed Life of Jorja Graham (Book 2)

Havenwood Falls Legend series
Trapped Within a Wish (Book 1)
Released from a Curse (Book 2)

Stand-alone Titles/Anthologies
Falling Out of Focus
The Crimson Countess
Fairy Tale Confessions - One Last Con (Anthology)

Prophecies of The Nine series
Entasy (Book 1)
Redemption (Book 2)
Devotion (Book 3) – Coming Soon

PARANORMAL ROMANCE AUTHOR
ROOTED IN MYTHOLOGY ⟞⟝ TWISTED INTO FANTASY

Brynn Myers

Made in the USA
Coppell, TX
05 April 2021

53151319R10156